A Different Heroism

Jane Lebak

A Different Heroism

Jane Lebak

Philangelus Press
Boston, MA USA

Cover art by Charlotte Volnek

One

In the middle of the Consecration, Father Jay's vision blacked out.

He said Eucharistic Prayer II so often for daily Mass that he had it memorized, so he focused on the words he knew ought to come next. He kept the panic from his voice, and he kept his eyes fixed where he knew the lectionary ought to be.

He closed his eyes to make the darkness feel more natural, but still he couldn't focus on the most sacred point of the Mass. The Eucharist was everything. He should be engaged in contemplating Christ's sacrifice, and instead he was tallying which of his parishioners at a Thursday-morning Mass worked as nurses, just in case the vision problem turned into numbness, weakness, and eventual collapse.

Two days of migraines had culminated in this. He couldn't go blind before turning thirty, could he? Jay paused in the vocal prayer and prayed inside, *I'm scared.*

When he opened his eyes, spots of grey swam out of the darkness, and then the world appeared as if through a filter. Finally his vision came back, all eighteen degrees of blur that he was thankful to God he had at all.

When Mass ended, Jay fought the urge to collapse onto the old couch in the corner of the St. Gus sacristy. Instead he fumbled off his green vestments in a hurry because in an hour, he had to say a funeral for a police officer. If anyone realized he felt this bad, they might stop him, and the deceased didn't deserve that.

Jay checked the time: his brother Kevin would pick him up in five minutes, so he hurried to hang up the vestments. As he was putting away the parish's dented chalice, two of the church ladies giggled behind him.

"You ask."

"I can't."

Jay turned, and the first said, "Fine, I will."

A shape swirled into view, and Jay recognized one of the daily Mass regulars. He shivered: she was just the type to have noticed his hesitation during the Consecration, or how his hands shook while distributing Communion.

She said, "Is it a sin to receive Communion without brushing your teeth?"

Jay blinked. "What?"

"Is it disrespectful to Jesus?" said the other lady. "To have bad breath or plaque?"

Of all the questions... Jay tried to get his bearings. "I don't see why it would be. The Eucharist is Christ under the appearance of bread and wine. It's not as if you cause Jesus pain when you chew the Host."

One of the women gasped. "The nuns told me never to chew the Host!"

Jay steadied himself. "Think about all the horrible things people say to one another with their mouths. That's a lot worse than a little plaque. I wouldn't worry."

"Speaking of things people say," said a voice that made Jay's skin crawl, "I wanted to ask about your homily today."

He didn't need vision to recognize Gary Stratowsky, a man in his mid-thirties whom Jay imagined had found a copy of the Catholic *General Instruction of the Roman Missal* and committed the entire thing to memory with a heart toward rooting out any and all liturgical abuse. ("Liturgical abuse" being a thing Jay had never heard of before Gary pointed it out.)

Jay pivoted toward him with a smile. "Sure, what about?"

Gary sounded triumphant. "The homily was two minutes long."

Whether or not it was in the GIRM, Gary believed every homily should last eight minutes, plus or minus two. Doubtless he carried a stopwatch.

Jay said, "I believe I mentioned the homily would be brief because I'm on my way to a funeral."

Gary probably carried a scorecard as well, marking off how many times Jay skipped the homily as a pastoral consideration. For example, the day temperatures had reached 105 degrees and somehow broken the laws of physics to reach 101% humidity, everyone should have marinated in puddles of sweat and offered it up as a sacrifice rather than Jay cutting everything short.

Gary took a lecturing tone. "Omitting the homily is allowed, but there's no regulation about shortening it."

Jay closed the closet door. "I made a judgment call, and I finished my point in two minutes. As it is, I'm cutting it close to get to the funeral." He picked up the white vestments he'd set aside, and he smiled at the blurred shape that was his regulation-loving tormentor. "We can talk later for the omitted six minutes if you'd like."

Gary said, "Shouldn't you use black vestments for a funeral?"

"Buy them for me," Jay said, "and I'll gladly use them to say yours."

Gary laughed, thank goodness. That could have gone all kinds of wrong, and Jay already regretted the words. Gary said, "That's a good idea! I should set aside funds to buy black vestments for my funeral Mass, since no one is likely to have any."

Jay walked past him to the door, and the church ladies said, "See you tomorrow," as they finished the clean-up.

In the parking lot, Jay located the smudge of his brother's car, and he moved toward it. Light glinted off the windows, and his head pounded. Talk about offering it up: the combination of Gary and a migraine had to equal two years' time served in Purgatory.

At the car, he leaned in the window. "I hope you weren't waiting long."

"A couple of minutes. I didn't want to bother you."

Jay bit back a remark about Catholic Cooties as he opened the back door to lay out his vestments. Although he and Kevin had an uneasy truce about their Big Disagreement, bringing it up in these circumstances wasn't in anyone's best interests. So instead, as Jay got into the front seat, he said, "I almost wished you'd been there to keep some of my parishioners away."

"You've got groupies." Kevin sounded amused, much better than sounding lectured. "Who'd have thought?"

As they drove, Jay looked at Kevin in his dress uniform. Kevin had never met the officer whose funeral they were attending, but police work created a brotherhood that made all of them feel one another's losses.

This situation was even more complicated. The officer hadn't been shot "in the line of duty." By all accounts it looked like a home invasion gone horribly wrong, but the police thought he'd been targeted. The officer's wife and child had been in the home, and the assailant had shot the woman. Shot her right in front of her kid.

The world wasn't right. Its wrongness had been part of what drove Jay to the priesthood in the first place, as though he could transfer from being a soldier for the army and become a soldier for God, hefting a Bible instead of a rifle to spread peace in his wake. And then when this happened, when a boy saw his mother gunned down in her own living room, Jay waded chest-deep into the sadness because that's what he'd enlisted to do.

His head pounded, and he rubbed his temples.

Kevin said, "Do you have your magic words ready?"

"I'm not the one giving the homily," Jay said, "so no."

They arrived at a church three times as big as St. Gus, airy and clean in a way that left Jay's eyes begging for darkness. In the sacristy he shook hands with Father Jordan, a priest he'd met a couple of times before at diocesan functions, and Father Jordan thanked him for coming even as Jay thanked him for the chance to concelebrate. Kevin hadn't asked him to do this, but since they'd reconciled at Christmas, Jay had naturally come into closer contact with the police force. Ten months was apparently enough time that when a Catholic officer died, the police chief wanted him to participate.

Father Jordan was nice enough to Jay, but even with his poor vision, Jay could tell the difference in the quality of their vestments. It shouldn't matter. Actually, it didn't matter. *Don't tell Gary,* Jay prayed, *but I bet you're not really hung up about the quality of our garments.* It just showed the difference when money flowed on tap and had done so for decades.

Father Jordan also didn't make a big deal about Jay's relative inexperience even though he'd been a priest since before Jay was born. He hunted through a cabinet for the preferred set of chalices and patens, and after he'd set aside three, Jay blurted out, "How many do you have?"

Father Jordan shook his head. "Too many. There's no way we can use them all, but whenever someone dies, we get another donation." He chuckled. "Don't you wish you could figure out how to turn them away? But the families want us to use the things."

Jay said, "You'll have to trust me, that's not a problem at St. Gus. We've got exactly one."

He powered through the funeral, shocked by how many people packed the church, how many dark blue uniforms showed up in his narrowed vision. This parish also had a deacon and a pastoral assistant—what would Jay give for either of those? Father Jordan delivered an excellent homily about hope in Christ (even without the help of Gary's stopwatch), but Jay said the prayer of the faithful with intentions he'd written himself, including one for the child Seth.

Afterward, Jay shook hands with more people than he could count, including Seth and the parents of the murdered couple, and forced himself not to look as ragged as he felt.

It wasn't even eleven. He had so much to do, and knives kept pushing through his skull.

Back in the sacristy, Father Jordan asked if Jay would attend at the graveside. Jay begged off. Kevin might want to go, but doubtless Jay could find his way home from here. He just didn't think he could stand for much longer without getting dizzy.

Father Jordan said, "Well, here, take this," and Jay heard a couple of clangs before feeling a paper bag pressed into his arms. Whatever was inside glinted a coppery-gold, and he blurted out, "Really?"

A chalice and paten set. New, gleaming, and undented.

Father Jordan laughed. "Why not? I'm sure the donors would rather they're used than getting rusty."

Jay managed a thank-you through the fog gathering in his head. Home. He craved home. It wasn't much, just a dark rectory with a basement apartment and a second floor filled with homeless kids, but it was a space to collapse at least momentarily.

Behind him, he heard, "Jay?"

The tension ebbed. "Ah, it's my ride."

Kevin chuckled. "Glad I've made my mark on the world. Are you ready to go to the graveside?"

"Actually, I'm not going. I planned to take the bus back."

Kevin sounded acidic. "Sure, I'll let you take two buses through three of the worst neighborhoods in the city. Then I get to go to *your* funeral."

"I live in one of the three, you realize." All the same, relief crawled through Jay. "But I don't want to keep you away."

"I've put in an appearance. Let's get out of here."

He ought to protest. He ought to say Kevin had intended all along to do more than "put in an appearance." But then again, in a perfect world he ought to be able to see clearly and walk without a limp, so Jay just said, "Thank you."

Two

In Kevin's professional opinion, Jay looked like death, and as a professional, Kevin had dealt with numerous dead bodies. Some of them had more color than Jay standing there in that sacristy. That's when Kevin made a command decision not to get Jay any closer to a grave than he already was.

He walked Jay out to the car slowly even though he was edgy to get out before the funeral procession, but then he found a back exit and cut past the lineup of cars.

In the passenger seat, Jay said very quietly, "Don't ever make me do that for you."

Sunlight streamed into the hot car, but Kevin got goosebumps. "What?"

"Your funeral. I don't want to say your funeral." Jay swallowed hard. "All those officers there as support, all the things they said about Officer Cantrel—I don't want to say them for you. You have to stay safe."

Kevin's hands tightened on the steering wheel. "It goes with the job, you know? But I'm not eager to die, so, sure." He hesitated. "Can you even do a funeral for a non-Catholic?"

Jay shrugged. "I could hold a memorial service, and I'd say Masses for the repose of your soul until the end of my life. I do that for Mom."

Kevin's brow furrowed. "Would you be allowed to say a funeral for Dad?"

"If he wanted a Catholic funeral, there's no reason I couldn't. That would be hard too. But..."

Kevin let him trail off. *But children are supposed to bury their parents.* There was so much Kevin could have said, and he didn't know how. He could have reminded Jay that they'd nearly buried him after he'd driven over a land mine in Iraq. He could have quipped that statistically speaking, one of them was pretty much bound to outlive the other.

He could have, but the note in Jay's voice was so plaintive that Kevin couldn't keep going. Didn't want to.

Jay kept going anyhow. "Whenever I hear sirens, I pray for you. Even if you don't think it means anything, I pray for you and for all our first responders."

Kevin's skin crawled. The light turned green. "Given your neighborhood, I may be the most prayed-for person on the planet."

Jay forced a smile. "Lucky you."

There was nothing to say to that, so Kevin kept driving. Skipping the graveside meant he'd have time enough to go home, eat lunch, and maybe get a nap before work. His tours now started at two in the afternoon and went until midnight.

Jay said, "What's that thing you guys say when an officer dies in the line of duty?"

Why did Jay have to keep talking about this? "It's 'Rest in peace, brother. We've got it from here.'"

Jay said, "It's a shared mission. It's as if the officer won't move forward unless he knows the job is going to get done."

Kevin bit his lip. "I guess you could look at it that way."

Jay sounded thoughtful. "But it's never finished, is it?"

Kevin flexed his hands on the wheel. "No. Not that I can see."

Jay finally stopped talking about it, and soon Kevin dropped him off at the curb outside the rectory. Hip hop music blasted out the second-floor windows, and Jay grimaced. "Thank you" he said, as though Kevin had done him some kind of big favor by getting him roped into holding a funeral for people he didn't know.

Kevin said, "Hey, your day off is what, Monday? Come over and I'll make dinner."

Jay's eyebrows raised. "You?"

"Yeah, me. Holly will be there too. I've got something I want you to try."

Jay looked amused, as well he should. "You bought the hot dogs *with the cheese already inside them*?"

"Ha-ha. So funny." Kevin rolled his eyes. "No, it's the jar of peanut butter with stripes of jelly around the edge, so you don't have to mess up two knives."

"Sounds good. I'll bring the bread with the crusts pre-cut." Jay grinned, and for the first time he looked alive. "What time?"

"Dinner. Holly said she can drive you. I'd invite your girlfriend," Kevin added, "but you haven't had one for a while."

"I'm married to the Church," Jay said as he shut the car door. "There's a billion Catholics, so I'll bring extra napkins." He laughed, looking right into Kevin's face with that unnerving focused stare he'd used ever since his vision went south. "I can't believe you've become some kind of gourmet chef."

"Don't believe it." Kevin shrugged. "I found something weird, and I think I can cook it."

"Now you've got me curious." Jay stepped back. "See you Monday."

Kevin lived twenty minutes from St. Gus, even less in the midday traffic. He'd gotten used to the roads between them during the past year, so while driving on autopilot, he found himself thinking about Richard Cantrel, gunned down in his own home. What a monstrous thing. What a monster who did it, human slime not even worth scraping off your shoe, deciding your life was an even exchange for his whatever grudge he held against you.

You accepted that at some point during police academy. You accepted that some people who benefitted from the laws you enforced might go ballistic if you ever caught them breaking one. You accepted potential hatred and misunderstanding and maybe even a bullet. But to have the guy invade your home and shoot your wife? No one signed up for that.

At his apartment complex, Kevin walked across the parking lot resenting this gorgeous day: the sunlight should have been occluded by thunderheads, and the central playground should have been empty of laughing children. Before heading upstairs he checked his mailbox, but instead of envelopes, he found a yellow slip saying his mail was held at the manager's office pending a signature.

He wasn't expecting a package. Maybe an enraged city dweller had mailed him a fish head.

At the office, he signed for a box a little too light and small to contain explosives, plus it was from his father in Florida. Dad had sealed it with enough packing tape to keep Office Depot's stock on the upswing until October, so Kevin didn't even try to open it until he reached his kitchen and could slide a steak knife through the brown paper.

It held a cardboard jewelry box, and inside that Kevin found an engagement ring.

Oh for heaven's sake—that wasn't just *an* engagement ring. That was *Mom's* engagement ring.

He fumbled open the letter, the words disconnecting so he couldn't understand what he was reading. But Dad wanted him to have this, apparently. *Dear Kevin,* it began, and the sentences wouldn't gel. *Jay was talking to me about your mother's wedding ring... ...never had a ring of my own... ...but it's just gathering dust... ...Jay said it would get stolen from him...*

Kevin stuffed the ring and the letter back in the package and walked away. He locked his sidearm in the gun safe, then stared out the window to watch the kids on the playground. After ten minutes, he made a cup of coffee, then turned on the TV, turned it off again, and returned to Dad's letter.

> *Dear Kevin,*
>
> *Jay and I were talking last week, and he asked whatever happened to your mother's wedding*

ring. It's been in a safety deposit box for the past twenty years because I couldn't bear to bury her with it, but then I wasn't sure what to do with it afterward.

I never had a wedding ring of my own, so I can't offer you that, but I thought maybe it's best to give her engagement ring to you. I've saved it all these years, but it's just gathering dust, and someday you might want to get married.

It's not heirloom quality, and it's not expensive enough that you'll have to pay a gift tax, but it has good memories. Jay said he couldn't use it and it would get stolen from him anyhow, and he thought you should have it. The ring is only 10 karat gold, but you could have the diamond reset if it can't be resized.

Let me know when you get this.

Love,

Dad

Kevin couldn't read between the lines at all on this one. Was Dad dating and he figured it was time to jettison the last memories of his wife? Was he trying to divest himself of anything of value so he could go on Medicaid? The whole letter amounted to little more than a receipt. Dad just should have written, *Enclosed please find ring,* and saved himself the trouble.

Kevin sat at the table with his coffee, staring at the diamond solitaire. Mom had picked a stone that was actually diamond-shaped, not heart-shaped or whatever they did with diamonds over at the mall. He'd never gone ring shopping. How would you even know the difference between a good stone and a lousy one?

And what about Mom's wedding ring, since Dad had started the letter with it? Kevin searched the packing material, but there wasn't a second ring, so Dad must have dug out the engagement ring, mailed it up north, and then did what with the wedding ring? Saved it in case Jay ever eloped with one of the church ladies?

He manipulated the ring in his fingertips so the light fragmented into rainbows on its different faces. It felt so small, a piece of metal around a hollow center where there was nothing, nothing holding it in shape, just time and hope.

Hope hadn't done squat for Richard Cantrel. Or for Lucy Cantrel, shot in her own living room.

And Dad wanted him to use this? Use it on Holly? Holly had never harmed anyone and didn't deserve what his father was asking for her. Late nights wondering if her husband was late because of paperwork or because of a gunshot, fear whenever the phone rang, fellowship with other wives and husbands who knew the same tension and dreaded the same pain.

Dad had never met her, but he wanted to condemn her?

Kevin glanced at the clock: time to head to work. He left the ring on the table while he retrieved his sidearm from the gun safe, but at the last second, he stopped. Leaving the safe open, he slid the ring back into its cheap cardboard box, then tucked it beside his box of ammunition. With the ring hidden in the far corner, he locked the door.

Three

Jay awoke on Friday with his jaw clenched and his face hurting. Terrific: he'd been frowning in his sleep again, not the best way to relax. In bed with the lights out, he said his morning prayers and steeled himself for the day. No funerals, but still too much.

In the kitchen, he flipped on the light and found himself looking at a cat.

It was a gorgeous animal, sitting on the kitchen table all black and gold-eyed like a miniature panther. There was only one problem: Jay didn't own a cat.

It took a moment to register what he was looking at, but that was quite definitely a cat, and quite definitely on his table. Finally Jay said, "What are you doing here?"

The cat didn't answer, fortunately. He'd begun to worry this was a modern day version of Balaam's ass where the animal was going to say out loud, *There's an angel about to strike you if you turn on the coffee maker.* So instead Jay said, "Which of the boys brought you in?"

When he moved toward it, the cat jumped off the table and left the room, so he followed, but it disappeared into the unfinished part of the basement. He'd have to get one of the boys to return the animal to wherever it belonged. There was already enough chaos in the rectory without bringing in wildlife.

By dawn, Jay was dressed and breakfasted and upstairs telling the resident homeless boys (well, used-to-be-homeless) to go get their cat out of the basement.

The boys all reassured him it wasn't their cat, that they hadn't brought in a cat, and no one would ever have dreamed of bringing in a cat, but since it was downstairs anyway, they all wanted to go see it.

"Just take it back to wherever you found it," he said. "We can't have a cat here."

Last December when he'd let the boys move into the unused upstairs, Jay hadn't really planned anything. It was cold; he had heat. They had no homes; he had space. Ever since his arrival at St. Gus, he'd been reaching out to the street kids, and that had been the natural next step.

They'd even organized a gang around the parish, calling themselves the Archangels. A mixture of homeless kids and those with homes but skating on the edge of subsistence, they kept the church grounds safe and helped out whenever they could, patrolling the parking lot and serving at the soup kitchen or anywhere else they were needed. The cops looked the other way because the kids weren't knifing one another or dealing drugs, and every now and then Jay got a scolding from the bishop's office. The arrangement was serviceable, even if it wasn't anything Jay had ever expected from the priesthood.

Another thing he hadn't expected: how the homeless kids would rotate in and out of the house. He'd figured, if you had a place to stay, you'd stay in it. Not necessarily. They'd drift in, spend a few weeks, maybe only a night, then drift out again to who-knows-where. Especially during the summertime, the second floor's population density varied from day to day quite a bit, and Jay forced himself not to ask too many questions about where they went on the nights they weren't here.

Also: they ate like there was no tomorrow. Even the ones who didn't linger could be counted on to raid the fridge.

So having one of them bring in a cat wasn't at all a shock; Jay was mostly surprised that it had taken so long and that it hadn't been a dog.

Those long-ago mornings suffused with quiet recollection, when Jay could gather his thoughts and meditate in preparation for the day: gone. Even on the least-populated days, a handful of teens produced thumps, shouts, laughter, door-slams, and cabinet bangs. A house rule kept the radios silent until Jay left to say daily Mass. Afterward, all bets were off. Usually you could hear yourself think.

Some of the kids scrambled to get ready for school (how you managed school with no home and no parents, Jay had no clue, but a few went some of the time.) Others headed out to wherever they spent the day loitering.

Another house rule demanded that long-term residents keep a part-time job, and Jay was proud to report a few success stories there. Two of the former residents had even scraped up first and last month's rent for an apartment.

By the time Jay returned from daily Mass, the last kid in the house reported that no cat remained on the premises. "It left through a window," said Esai.

Jay studied him. "Aren't you supposed to be at school?"

"I'll get there before lunch." Esai smirked at him, but he was wearing the Municipal Catholic Middle School uniform, so he probably did intend to go. "Maybe."

Esai was one of the throwaways. He had family in the area, but so far Jay had seen them only after he'd gotten the kid enrolled in the Catholic school. A couple of irate women had shown up at the rectory screaming that he'd better not go baptizing the kid, because they knew all about *those Catholics*. Catholics apparently played with sorcery by baptizing unsuspecting infants, but their food and housing was okay. No, Esai's extended family hadn't wanted him back. His mother was in prison and his father was...well, somewhere.

"Sister Magdalena is going to meet you at the school with a clipboard," Jay said. "Get in there before she gives you detention."

Esai headed for the front door, but he said, "She won't give me detention, man. I'm a rock star."

Nodding, Jay went into his office where the parish secretary, Mrs. D, immediately held out a pink message slip. "The bishop called. He'd like you to call back."

Oh, what a joy this could be. "Did he give any hint why?"

"None at all." Mrs. D smiled. "He's always nice on the phone, though."

So, let's tally up the possibilities. Jay might have won a citation from Rome and they were flying out a world-class chef with a year's supply of food for the Caf. His dear parishioner Gary might also have called one time too many and Jay was about to get nailed to the wall for short homilies on days he had to concelebrate a funeral.

At his office, he found the door already open. Mrs. D called, "Your first visitor got here early, so I let him in to wait for you." She pointed to the coffee maker. "And if you push the button behind you, something magical will happen."

"I'm on it." Jay pushed the switch, then stepped into his office where a very tattooed man lurked by his desk.

All the hair stood on Jay's arms. The guy loomed over him and shook Jay's proffered hand with a grip firm enough that Jay felt like a rag doll. The visitor had piercing dark eyes and long hair tied behind his neck, and Jay almost could remember his name.

The man spoke with a hesitancy at odds with his physique. "Is it all right if I talk to you?"

That voice also evoked a name just beyond reach. Jay forced a steady tone. "Why wouldn't it be all right?"

This happened too often: a good thing that he hated. But he couldn't visibly shudder. He couldn't run. This was nothing more than the natural consequences of having lived the life he'd lived before God had pulled him up by the scruff of his neck.

Jay could tell the man's story without the man even speaking, a story this man probably thought unique unto himself—and only Jay would understand because Jay had been a street kid too. A gang member, a hooligan, and a thief. The kind of kid that kept Kevin in a job. He'd gotten out before it had turned into all-out thuggery and organized crime. The ones who didn't? Well, they slunk into his office while he was off saying daily Mass. They edged in the front door without an appointment or snuck into the back row at Mass or lurked for him in the parking lot after dark.

And then they'd confess to him every atrocity they'd ever done, the moment it had gone too far, the heartbreaking chances they'd had to turn back but didn't, the loved ones they'd hurt with their inevitable drug addictions and hair-trigger tempers. They'd ask what to do, how to return from that. They'd ask if God still loved them.

Jay would have to listen, knowing with every word that if not for the grace of God, he'd be doing much worse things right now, assuming he wasn't already knifed and left for dead.

The man said, "Do you know who I am?"

Jay closed the door and sat in the adjacent chair. "You're a child of God."

The man swallowed hard. "I can't be."

Trying not to flinch, Jay listened as the man detailed horrors. His heart pounded. And as he talked to the man (who gave his name as Mitch) Jay reminded himself that Jesus said there was more joy in heaven over one conversion than over ninety-nine saintly lives. Reminded himself repeatedly. He pressed his palms against his legs to prevent his hands from shaking. *Your brother was dead, but now is alive,* Jesus had recounted in a parable, but Jay found that theoretical joy so far from what his heart told him whenever this happened. He prayed and tried not to hear too much.

He kept telling himself, *Right now, I* am *the Catholic Church. I am the face of God. If I turn my back, he's truly hopeless.*

He'd been hopeless like this too, years ago when his broken body had lain in a hospital bed and his broken soul had struggled to drag itself toward the light.

Now wasn't the time to look at the clock, and Jay didn't pay attention to the noises in the main office. It was just him and a soul, one on one, a man who eventually broke down in tears and asked if any of that could ever be forgiven, and if so, why? Why would God let him do all that and then take him back, and how could he ever make up for it?

"We don't make up for it." Jay leaned forward and looked him right in the eye. There was a tissue box on the desk, but he'd been trained over and over never to hand them to people, in case they thought tears were shameful. "Christ made up for it. We give God the only things we can, our love and our faith and our resolution to try again."

The man stared at his lap. "That's not enough. I told you what I did."

Jay put a hand on his shoulder. "Don't try to pay for what's freely given."

It turned out the man had been raised Catholic and had gotten almost up to his Confirmation, so Jay offered to make this his Confession.

The man's head jerked up. "You can do that?"

Jay nodded "If you want to come home, do it now. In this office, before you give yourself an excuse not to. We'll count anything we already talked about as having been brought before God for forgiveness, and anything else you can remember to confess. If you think of anything later that you forgot, you can take care of it then."

The man's voice cracked. "I'd like that."

Ten minutes later, Jay felt as if he'd run a marathon, but the man in front of him sported a squeaky-clean soul and bloodshot eyes. "I'll come back. I'll be here Sunday. I sent my kids to Catholic school, but I never dared. I wanted to come back so long now." Mitch paused, then added, "I didn't think you'd do it. I thought you'd turn me away."

Jay took a deep breath, then reached forward and embraced the man.

The man hugged him with a bone-crushing grip, but Jay only thanked God another life had turned around.

In Mrs. D's office, Jay asked her to make an appointment for Mitch next week, just to check in, and then picked up his messages. Naturally the bishop had called again. He turned to get his hour-old coffee and found a boy ghosting by the coffee machine.

It took a moment before he recognized him. "Seth Cantrel?"

With folded arms, the kid glared at the ground. He was twelve, his bedraggled hair a shade too long and his eyes shadowed. And he was fifteen miles from home at a time when he should have been in school.

Jay puzzled. "Did your grandparents bring you? Do you want to talk?"

"No." He still hadn't met Jay's eyes, and he shifted his feet. "Whatever. I just wanted to see where you were."

He walked out of the office. Jay followed the kid into the dimly-lit hallway and from there out the front door.

As Seth jumped down the porch steps, Jay called, "At least stay for lunch."

The kid shook his head.

Jay added, "It's not glamorous, but you could help with the cooking."

Seth turned around. "Do I look like some kind of chef?"

Jay said, "My vision's not that good, so I wouldn't know."

Seth snorted. "Well, I'm not."

"Then you can set the tables. Come on." Jay edged down the steps and headed toward the church building. "The cafeteria is in the basement, and I've got ninety people coming for lunch."

He had no idea if Seth would follow, but shortly the kid said, "You having a party?"

"Every day's a party. Today it's chili with elbow macaroni and a bathtub-sized quantity of apple crisp. You don't need to be a master chef to slice apples."

Seth didn't reply, but Jay kept walking. At the church, he unlocked the door opening to the parish hall in the basement. Footsteps at his back reassured him Seth still followed, so he flipped on the lights before making his way into the kitchen.

Seth waited at the door. Jay said, "Help me with the pots."

It went on like that, Jay never sure if Seth would leave. But one step at a time, Seth involved himself in the soup kitchen's prep work. Volunteers arrived, and they'd introduce themselves to Seth only to get no response, so Jay just said, "This is Seth," and they left it at that.

The lunch rush started. Seth served up big spoonfuls of apple crisp and delivered them to the tables. After half an hour, he stopped returning to the kitchen, and Jay hoped that meant he had decided to eat something too. Then, before the end of the meal, Jay scarfed down one of the leftover bowls of chili and climbed back up to the parking lot.

"Hey, man! I thought I'd have to come in for you." It was Spider, one of Jay's success stories, and a car needing enough repairs that you could only barely call it a success. "You ready to go?"

"Give me five minutes."

Jay went into the rectory to grab a book, and when he stepped inside, Mrs. D rushed up to him. "We have a problem. It's Enrique Hoyos."

Jay's mouth opened. "Oh no—" He and Enrique had worked together at Our Lady Queen of Angels. Jay had been an associate pastor and Enrique a parishioner who ran the OLQA youth group and the liturgy committee, but they hadn't seen each other in two and a half years.

"He's okay." Mrs. D lowered her head. "His family scraped together money for his mother to come visit from Ecuador. Only she died suddenly during her visit. OLQA will donate the funeral services, but even with the funeral home cutting them a discount, they don't have the money to bury her here or to send her body home. OLQA wanted to know if we could help."

A ringing began in Jay's ears. "And you told them we could." Mrs. D nodded. Jay ventured further. "How much do they need?"

"Three thousand dollars."

The blood drained from his head. He was already doing the math.

Mrs. D froze. "Wait a minute. We just paid all the bills, didn't we?"

Jay waved her down. "Don't worry. I'd have said the same."

Mrs. D rushed to the desk and pulled out the parish checkbook, but Jay spoke before she got to the right page. "$254.72."

"Close. $257.42." Tremulous, she looked up. "Is there anyone we can ask?"

Jay didn't roll his eyes and suggest she check the garden for a newly-blossoming money tree. "I asked all of our large donors last week to keep the Caf open. No one's got a dollar to spare."

Shaking her head, Mrs. D bit her lip. "What do we do?"

"We pray." Jay went into his office and grabbed the book off his desk. "But right this minute, I've got an appointment, and my ride is waiting."

Four

In a sterile office, Jay sat on the opposite side of a doctor's desk, glaring at the far wall. They'd finished up in the exam room, and Dr. Lacks had told him to get dressed and come talk where it was more friendly-like.

Hah. Lacks had reviewed every one of Jay's trouble-spots: his eyes, his reflexes, and finally his heart and lungs. At every point, even though Jay had made the appointment himself and come in voluntarily, he had to remind himself to answer honestly. Even eight years and ten thousand mortifying medical questions after blowing himself up in Iraq, he still had the urge to run rather than talk to a doctor.

Dr. Lacks pored over his medical records. "You're right, Father Farrell. We needed to talk."

It was too late to run. "What's the verdict?"

"Diagnosis is this: you correctly identified that you're in terrible shape. The one good thing is that you haven't lost any more weight. But your vision is deteriorating too rapidly for my peace of mind, and your nerves aren't responding properly. This isn't anything new. It's all the Iraq injuries acting up again."

Jane Lebak

Jay said, "Why?"

"I can make an educated guess," Dr. Lacks said blandly. "It's one in the afternoon and you look as if you're ready to turn in for the night."

Jay chuckled. "I just finished work in the Caf. That's pretty intense."

"And before that?"

"The whole day's been intense, really."

"And yesterday?"

Jay twisted the ring on his finger, a new addition to his priest uniform. "Yesterday I had a funeral in the morning and the Caf at noon, and then the bereavement support group and the finance committee meeting, plus a prayer service after dinner and the youth group. I know what you're implying. But what can I do about it?"

Dr. Lacks looked incredulous. "There isn't a pill or a procedure, Father Farrell. I think you know that."

Jay glowered. "Spell it out."

"You need to do less. You drove over a land mine and failed to die, but that doesn't mean you're invulnerable. It does mean you need to take better care of yourself than the average person. You joke about having the body of a man twice your age, but despite that, you're working yourself to death."

Jay shrugged. "Honestly, I don't have a choice."

Dr. Lacks said, "And honestly, I don't see that you have any other choice than to slow things down."

Jay drummed his fingers against his leg. "Is there a vitamin or a therapy or a drug?"

"Overmedication is malpractice the way unnecessary surgery would be, and at any rate, there's nothing I can do. And there's nothing you can do. There are things you can *not* do, and you have to begin not doing them." Dr. Lacks leaned closer. "You should start by getting eight hours of sleep a night and taking reasonable breaks during the day. Get a gym membership and do some light exercise."

Jay shook his head. "My parish needs me."

Dr. Lacks steepled his fingers. "What did you suspect when you came to me?"

Jay froze in place.

"At the very least, right now you're in such shape that I highly recommend you take a week of sick leave."

Jay frowned. "I'm scheduled up the hilt. Maybe in November."

Dr. Lacks leaned into the desk. "Look at me." It was a low voice, a no-nonsense voice that barely carried across the desk and therefore riveted Jay's attention. "I want you to listen to what I have to say, because I'm not joking."

Two minutes later, Jay exited Dr. Lacks' office, white as a sheet.

Paperwork wasn't the best part of the day, but it was the most predictable. Kevin could fill out arrest forms with his eyes closed if he needed to, and some nights he'd pulled so much overtime that he pretty much did.

Tonight's collar was drug-related, of course. Some guy who needed his fix decided on a payday advance (of course) by snatching someone's wallet. There were credit cards in it (of course) so a misdemeanor instantly became a felony (of course) and a half-hour high was about to turn into a several-month low.

A shadow loomed over the desk. Kevin didn't bother to look at the man casting it. "What's up?"

His partner said, "They found Cantrel's killer."

Kevin's head shot up. "Really?"

Bill stood with his arms folded. "You're not going to like it."

"I don't like it already." Kevin's brow furrowed. "Or do you mean the perp accidentally fell down the stairs during the arrest and landed in an inconveniently-placed meat grinder?"

"We're not that lucky." Bill was a solid black man with a square jaw and ripped arms that made him fill the space everywhere he went. "He's in a lockup over at the 23rd, and the worst thing that happened to him was he arrived in time for lunch."

Kevin braced himself. "So what else am I not going to like?"

Bill handed him a rap sheet, and Kevin jumped straight to the bottom.

The last entry was a regular traffic stop. Cantrel had cited the perp for driving without a license.

The killer (he assumed it was the killer) had been on police radar since age ten, all misdemeanor offenses and always given probation or a small fine or time served. He lived with his mother (well, until lunchtime today). He was seventeen.

"I hope he doesn't get tried as a juvenile," Kevin muttered. But then he realized what Bill had meant.

This was the motive. A moving violation.

Kevin could write the rest of the story: the kid goes and tries to get a job and it requires a valid drivers license, only he can't get it because of the violation. And then, high or drunk but filled with blame for the cop who ruined his life by catching him in the act of breaking the law, he went on social media and tracked him down.

And then boom.

Revenge, sure. It was revenge, but revenge for this? For something that hardly mattered? Something that if this loser had just waited a year and cleaned up would have been a funny story to tell his kids at a backyard barbecue?

Kevin swallowed hard. "You're sure about the meat grinder?"

Bill said, "Yeah."

Kevin shoved the chair back from his desk and walked away from the paperwork, his gun heavy in his belt. A traffic stop. A seventeen year old.

At seventeen, he'd been wild too, but it never would have occurred to him to stake out a cop's house and shoot his wife. Sure, he'd been in a gang, but on the bottom rung you didn't really think about murder. Maybe it was the guy's drugs (the killer had a few misdemeanors with those too) because drugs messed up what little common sense these bottom-dwellers possessed in the first place.

They just snapped. Like this kid with a rap sheet who just...lost perspective.

Kevin paced to the water cooler and then returned without any water. At the edge of the hallway stood Bill, arms folded.

Kevin met his eyes. Bill said, "Senseless."

"How could we have known?" Kevin said. "There has to be a way to catch people like that before they lose it so completely. I've seen a hundred rap sheets just like that one, but most of them turn into people who don't file their taxes and get into fights at tailgates in the stadium parking lot. Not premeditated murder."

Bill only nodded.

Kevin shivered. "There's got to be a way to net them before there's no turning back. Uproot them. Do something."

Bill said, "Preemptive vengeance doesn't really work. *Do unto others before they do unto you.*"

"I'm not talking about jailing them. I'm talking about rehabilitating them before they fall down the well."

Bill smirked. "Prehab."

Kevin said, "Yeah. Get the kid a mentor. Give him a job. Make him mentor someone else." He paused a moment. "Whatever keeps them out of juvy. Keep all of them busy enough that they've got no time to stew in their own resentment."

Bill folded his arms. "Sounds like a plan. I wonder what the chief would say."

Kevin laughed. "Yeah, I'll go suggest that. Actually, you suggest it. When's your sergeant exam?"

"Not for three months." Bill's eyes wrinkled. "You could take it too, you know."

Kevin huffed. "I'm good where I am."

"You've got ideas. The brass, they don't really like ideas."

"Then I really shouldn't take that exam, should I? But you can become the brass and use mine. I'm not really a study-for-the-exam type. Besides," and he grinned, "you've got that whole wife-and-family thing where you need the higher pay grade."

Bill shook his head. "You're good people, Farrell."

"I haven't filled out the paperwork to qualify for that." Kevin went past Bill back to his desk. The killer's rap sheet was still there, and Kevin thrust it back at Bill. The key might be in that list of petty violations and court appearances. But he'd never find it, and he'd only grow bitter hunting for the key to an unopenable lock.

Five

Jay would not think about what the doctor said. He would *not* think about it.

Instead Spider obliged Jay's need for insulation without even knowing about it, all but glowing with pride over his just-above-minimum-wage job that was almost able to keep him afloat in a roach-infested apartment along with a roommate bringing home just about as much.

Back at the rectory, Mrs. D handed him a message slip: the bishop called again.

"He didn't happen to offer three grand, did he?"

She looked pained. "I didn't ask."

Jay left another message with the chancery. The bishop's secretary must be used to his voice by now.

As he hung up, a shadow appeared at the door, and Jay focused until he could see a member of the Archangels gang. "Hey, man," said the boy, "I heard you need three big ones?"

Jay went cold. "It's okay, Esai. God will find it."

"I can put the word out for you."

"Seriously, Esai, nothing like that."

"Look, you're a good guy." Esai's voice hadn't changed yet, but thirteen wasn't too young to steal a car and bring it to the local chop shop. "If you say you need money, it's for something good."

"Where the money comes from *does* matter." Jay dropped his voice to a sterner tone. "I don't want anyone contributing money they can't declare on their income tax. If you give me three thousand dollars, I'm calling the cops. You agreed to the house rules when you came to stay."

Esai shrugged. "Your call." And he disappeared from the doorway.

Really, Jay should just text Kevin right now and send a squadron of cops. He wasn't long enough removed from the street that he didn't know exactly what Esai was thinking: loyalty. If your pals needed something, you got it for them because you had each others' backs. If Jay had been blessed with a mentor back then, and that mentor had needed three thousand, Jay would already have figured out how to separate that much money from someone who didn't need it as much. *They won't even miss it,* he'd have told himself. *Their insurance company will pick up the tab, and they'll get something even better than this. Who knows how they even got this in the first place—probably stole it themselves. We deserve it more.*

He was so tired, but he had to nip this in the bud so he didn't walk in tomorrow to find a roll of hundred dollar bills on the desk.

Jay trudged into the hallway and saw a gold gleam. When the image resolved, it took a while to register what he was seeing.

The black cat's shining eyes. That made two reasons to talk to the boys.

On the top floor, the boys were having a hushed discussion that ended abruptly when they saw him. It was almost comic. Almost. If you didn't consider the "mortal sin" side of things.

"No," Jay said.

"Don't be a moron," Esai said. "We can help you."

"No. No money from you guys." Jay folded his arms. "And no cat. Get that cat out of here."

The boys all swore they hadn't brought the cat back into the building. They promised they were not in the slightest, even a little, responsible for the presence of a cat.

"Well go down and get it out of here anyway," Jay said. "And no money."

"But why?" That voice was Masa's, and he didn't live here. Although younger than many of the Archangels, he was one of their movers and shakers. "You never ask us for nothing, man, so let us do this."

Jay said, "I don't ask you for anything because that's not why I let you stay here. You needed a place to stay. Fine. Christ said that on the last day, we're going to answer for how we helped others as if we helped Christ himself."

Masa sounded victorious. "So let us help you! It's for Christ!"

"Doesn't work that way," Jay said. "If you steal from someone to help me, you're also stealing from Christ himself."

Masa shrugged. "So it evens out. You steal from Christ and then give it back to Christ. He doesn't need money in Heaven anyhow."

This conversation wasn't at all working out the way Jay wanted it to.

Esai laughed out loud. "I'm okay with that."

"I'm not," Jay retorted. "I don't want anyone lifting a car or picking pockets. If God wants this done, it'll get done."

Masa said, "I've got this awesome trick, man, and no stealing. This professional wrestler showed up at the Boys and Girls Club thing, and he said if you cut your own forehead right here," (he pointed) "that you'll totally gush with blood. If I fall over in the mall and do that, I bet they'd give me three grand!"

Jay stared. "You're not serious, are you?"

"I'd do it, totally. So what you need the money for?" Masa said.

Jay sighed. The boys counted on him to be straight with them, and they knew garbage when they heard it, so he just put it out there. "My friend needs it for his mother's funeral."

The boys went completely silent. Probably compiling a mental catalog of the neighborhood automobiles.

"She was visiting from Ecuador," Jay went on. "He doesn't have the money to bury her, and St. Gus said we'd give it to him, but the problem is, we don't have it either."

"And it's three grand to bury someone?" one of the boys exclaimed. "They keep soaking you even after you're dead?"

Jay sighed. "It's their last chance to wring money from a stone."

Esai said, "Man, what do *you* charge to say a funeral?"

Jay said, "That's voluntary, and OLQA is donating the funeral. But I'm not selling coffins, and I'm not running a crematorium. I assume those businesses have expenses too."

Esai said, "Crooks."

As he said this, Jay noticed the kid standing behind Esai. Seth Cantrel.

He'd come back. And here Jay was talking about paying for a friend's mother's funeral. Nice job. He might as well have said, "Go steal a car tonight. Steal two if it helps."

Jay squinted at him. "Seth, do you need to call someone to come get you?"

"He's staying here," Masa said.

Jay said, "He's got a family and a home."

Esai said, "And he's staying here. What's the big deal?"

"The big deal is your grandparents are going to panic because you didn't come home." Jay pointed to the steps. "Use the office phone. Make sure they know where you are and that you're safe."

After a glare, Seth stomped down the steps.

Masa said, "Like it's so awesome to have a family."

"Dude," Esai snapped, "you're lucky you have a mother."

Masa huffed. "Yeah, so lucky. She yells about everything I do and everything I say."

Esai shot back, "And you're lucky. You have no clue."

As Esai stormed down the stairs, Jay called, "No grand theft auto."

Esai shouted back, "If that money ain't here, on the table, by Monday, I'm getting it for you."

Downstairs, the door slammed.

Jay's head pounded. Relaxation. Of course. Because in the face of this, you could just...relax.

Masa huffed. "Don't listen to Esai. He's just pissed because we got into a fight after school. These losers are trying to start their own loser gang at school, and we shut them down."

Jay rubbed his temples. "You can't do that."

"It's not like we cut anyone. Just made sure they know who's in charge. Sent them home crying." He laughed. "But that kid Seth is really cool. I'd let him in."

Jay shook his head. "Nothing illegal, Masa. Keep it that way."

"Nothing illegal. But if one of them hits me in the hallway," and here Masa grinned, "I'm totally blading my forehead and getting them expelled."

Downstairs Jay found his phone occupied by Seth, talking to someone in tones so low that Jay couldn't hear him at all. He shut his office door, then dropped into his chair.

He would not think about what the doctor had said. He wouldn't think about it. But his vision was cloudy, and his head ached so much.

Kevin stared at the phone number as though his glare could burn the letters into ash that would then drift away and prevent him from placing the call.

When that didn't happen, he leaned back in the passenger seat of the police cruiser and dialed.

Bill was talking to a few kids on the corner. *No, Officer, we're not doing anything, we have no idea why someone called and said someone was setting off fireworks, no we would never do that.*

Kevin liked watching Bill interact with the kids. It was a kind of positive reinforcement that would help them think of the cops more as a part of their community than as random enforcers to be feared and despised. Bill would make a good sergeant, no question.

A man answered the phone, so Kevin went into Official Police Mode to introduce himself by name and precinct, complete with his official voice (deeper and more enunciated).

The man sounded cautious. "Yes?"

"You are Richard Cantrel's father, correct?" When the man confirmed, Kevin said, "I'm terribly sorry for your loss. I'm calling about your grandson, Seth."

"What about him?"

"He's run away from home." Usually calls about runaways went in the other direction. "He showed up at a shelter earlier today and stated his intention to move in."

"What'd he do that for? We moved him here."

Kevin bristled at the man's annoyance. "We didn't interrogate him. It's preferable to keep a runaway in a safe harbor rather than risk him fleeing to avoid questions." This was the man's own grandson—

shouldn't he at least be concerned? "For now he's got a roof over his head and regular meals." Jay probably fed the kids, right? "But we think it would be best if all of us could meet with him to discuss why he ran away."

"Look, I don't have time for this!" The man huffed. "My son just died. My wife is out of her mind with grief, and I can't be spending all day molly-coddling a brat who wants everything just the way he wants it. The world doesn't give you a free ride, and it's high time he learned."

Outside the squad car, Bill was tossing a basketball with the kids. They were laughing.

"He's not a baby," the grandfather went on. "If Seth wants to run off, there's nothing I can do about it, and he can just suck it up and see what it's like on the street."

Kevin went into full Official Police Mode. "He's at Saint Augustine's Catholic Church, in case you or your wife want to check on him. Write down the phone number."

He made the man repeat it back to make sure he actually copied it, then thanked him for his time and disconnected the call.

Kevin should call Jay, but he had no idea what words would come out if he tried to speak. That man. That man…

Finally he sent a text. *Seth will be with you for a while.* Any more than that and he couldn't trust himself.

Six

In the middle of the 5PM Saturday Mass, a drunk guy showed up.

"Showed up" wasn't quite the right descriptor. Jay was giving the homily (nine and a half minutes on the dot, thank you Doctor of Theology Gary) when the man limped up the center aisle. When the guy got halfway up, he started shouting.

"God doesn't..." He gathered himself, then kept going, "It's not... This isn't right..."

Jay stopped talking, unsure whether to engage. The first rule of angry disruptions was not to escalate the situation, and the presence of anyone in a uniform (including a priest) would escalate things right off the bat. On the other hand, the man had sought out a Catholic church in the middle of Mass for his rant, so he must have wanted the priest to respond.

The man leaned on one of the pews. "God doesn't care. He never cared. It's not like that."

Jay studied him: the filthy, ill-fitting jeans, the battered sneakers, the way he wore two long-sleeve shirts one over the other even though it was September. Disheveled hair and an unshaved beard.

Homeless? Possibly. Maybe he had a home and hadn't returned to it for a couple of days.

Raising a fist, the man looked directly at Jay. "And you! You're a thief and a vandal! You went to war and murdered people! And you stand there talking about God! How stupid do you think we are?"

A spike of pain went through Jay's skull. His vision blurred.

"You're lying to everyone!" the man raged. "You broke windows! You shot people!"

Jay leaned on the lectern, but before he could speak, two shapes emerged out of the congregation.

"Take it easy," the first parishioner was saying. "Gear down, man. It's not worth it."

The drunk man bellowed, "Maybe God should just strike me down!"

The parishioner replied, "Hey, be respectful. You're in a church."

"Out of here," said the second. He put a hand on the drunk guy and started guiding him out.

Jay couldn't do more than watch as they escorted him outside. At the back door they were joined by a third really big guy.

When the man was out the door, he said, "Let's scrap the rest of that homily, shall we?"

He made his way out from behind the lectern and hoped his balance didn't go the way of his vision. The portable mic carried his unsteady voice. "None of you are shocked by that. You all know who I was." Kevin hated that he talked to them about his past, but Kevin wasn't here. "As a teen, I was a vandal and a thief. And

I did enlist in the army, and I did go to war, and I did shoot people. I'm not sure I ever hit anyone."

His body was unsteady too, so Jay made his way to one of the seats. A parishioner slid over so he'd have room. Gary could add this to his list of offenses. Pivoted halfway around on the bench, he faced back into the congregation. "I've always been honest about this: I was and still am a sinner. They're different sins nowadays, and I'm trying harder, but I'm a sinner. Back then I was dead. Morally, spiritually dead."

People were normally quiet during homilies, but the current silence crowded close around him like rush hour commuters. "I broke windows. I broke promises. I broke people." Jay swallowed hard. "We'd hot-wire a car and go for a joyride, and maybe we'd leave the car where the owner could find it. We'd drink and spray paint shop windows and hold up strangers at knifepoint, and all along, my soul was lifeless and disgusting, and God loved me anyhow."

He couldn't see a thing, so he closed his eyes and fought to steady himself. "When I preach about mercy, I want you to believe me. I lived it. I deserved death. I deserved to go to Hell, and I'd be there right now if God hadn't saved my life and then dragged me up out of that pit, with me clawing and screaming in protest the whole way up."

Jay looked around. Everyone was watching. "Pray for the man who was in here a few minutes ago. Pray for me. Pray for mercy for all of us because, in the end, God's mercy is the only thing that matters."

After Mass, Jay found two very large men hanging around near the statue of Saint Joseph, laughing with a comfort that Jay longed for. He'd felt it years ago in the gang. He'd felt it in seminary. And now, in the line of fire, he wished for it again.

One of the men said, "We took care of things."

"Thank you." Jay shook their hands. They were former gang members, and Jay strongly suspected they'd belonged to rival gangs. Not here: here in the Church, they were brothers with the same Father.

The second man said, "We took him off the property and made sure he didn't come back, but we'll walk you back to the rectory."

Jay started. "Was he armed?"

"He didn't have a gun. Might have had a knife," said one.

"I'd be surprised if he didn't," said the second.

The first one said, "The guy's an animal."

"No, not an animal." Jay let out a long breath. "You don't do something like that unless once, a long while ago, you really loved God."

His two criminal guards escorted him back to the rectory, although Jay figured the drunk guy was sleeping it off somewhere, or maybe ranting on a street corner about the evils of Christianity. He could hear the upstairs music from across the parking lot.

Two of the Archangels met him on the front porch. "Anything wrong, Farrell?"

"They took care of it." Jay turned to his bodyguards. "Thank you again."

"Man," Esai muttered. "We miss all the good stuff."

"That's why you need to come to Mass," Jay said dryly. "It's where all the good stuff happens."

The music was on way too loud, but the aching in his head made the stairs too steep to climb. Instead he asked Esai to tell them to turn it down.

So tired. He'd rest for a bit, cobble together something for dinner, and then turn in early. His doctor would have approved of that part, at least.

The phone rang before he could put any of that into action. Jay trudged into the office to answer it. "St. Augustine's."

"Jay Farrell! At last I reached you. You're answering your own phones now."

Jay retorted, "We did away with the secretary. It's cheaper like this. Plus I got her life insurance policy." He sat on the edge of the desk and rubbed the bridge of his nose. "I'm glad we finally got hold of each other, Bishop Sato."

Bishop Sato sounded happy. "You're an incredibly busy man. How are you holding up?"

Jay sighed. "Things keep working out, somehow."

"Hmm." The bishop paused momentarily. "There's something I need to talk to you about."

Jay humphed. "Are you about to scold me for my heretically short homilies?"

"Short? Usually folks complain because they're too long." The bishop laughed. "I'm guessing God has blessed you with a chance to learn patience in the form of one particular parishioner. I've dealt with that type too."

Jay's brow furrowed. "Then why the phone tag?"

"I'd rather explain in person. You don't need an appointment. Just drop by sometime next week."

"You're moving me?" Jay's heartbeat skipped. "What have I done wrong?"

"Nothing—nothing, Jay. You're not needed anywhere else right now. Don't think twice about it, but just make sure you drop in."

Whatever happened during the rest of the call, Jay couldn't remember it by the time he hung up. The upstairs music had edged down in volume, so he called it good enough.

In the basement, he flipped on the light in his bedroom and found his chair occupied by that cat.

"Get out of here!" he exclaimed. "Go. Now."

The cat stared at him, and Jay sighed. The boys were carrying this too far. Except his door had been locked— how had they gotten in? No, don't ask that. They all knew how to force a lock, but still, part of the deal was that they left his apartment alone unless invited. No pranks. They knew that.

He stared at the cat, who stared back at him.

Jay said, "Where did you come from, anyhow?"

He should chase the cat out. He really should. But he was so tired, and instead he staggered to his bed and dropped onto the mattress. Maybe in a while his head would stop throbbing. Maybe then he'd go upstairs and tell the boys to knock it off with the poor cat.

He must have dozed, because he startled awake to a much darker room, and when he sat up, the cat was gone.

Seven

A call came over the radio about a robbery Monday morning, so Kevin and Bill headed out. Convenience store. The first person he interviewed said the perp was a tall kid wearing a hoodie.

I'll get right on that and call in half the city for questioning.

Bill reviewed the surveillance footage while Kevin interviewed the witnesses and radioed in a slightly more thorough description. Another pair of officers talked to anyone on the street who might have seen the perp.

The perp had taken money but nothing else. At least Kevin could understand that. The worst were the crimes where the person stole food to go with the money (since Kevin assumed their personal budget earmarked all income under "Drugs.") When addiction got too bad, eating became optional. Jay probably fed a few of those in his parish, which had to be doing wonders for the neighborhood.

"You've got to see this," Bill called.

The perp did, indeed, have a hoodie and a gun. He also had a serious case of being a child.

"They start them young these days," Kevin said. "Did Dad send him out to pick up a pack of cigarettes, oh and while you're out, see if you can get someone to stuff this bag with twenties?"

Bill radioed in the description, and the other two officers came in. "Sick," Kevin muttered. "What is he, ten years old?"

"A regular child prodigy." One of the other two officers looked over Kevin's shoulder at the screen. "Probably learned at his father's knee."

"Give him more credit than that. They come up with these things on their own. We raided a middle school the other day," the fourth officer said. "Brought in the dogs. They thought they were in dog heaven from the sheer number of guns we pulled out of lockers."

Kevin's eyes widened.

Bill said, "That's why we've got to reach out to them early."

Kevin said to the other guys, "He's studying for the sergeant's exam. It's always like this."

Bill said, "Yeah, actually listening to you. Your next partner isn't going to do that."

He laughed, but Kevin realized all at once: he didn't want Bill to pass the sergeant's exam.

Kevin pushed back the urge. Bill would be a great sergeant. He was an amazing cop and would do the city proud, and not just as a sergeant. Heck, if Bill eventually became chief of police, the city could hardly do better, and Kevin would be proud to serve under him. But for just a moment, having Bill pass that exam was the worst thing in the world. Bill, in another precinct, doing another job, and Kevin here without him.

What would life look like in another couple of years? No Bill. Holly certainly wouldn't still be his girlfriend in two years—she'd either want to get married or move on. Dad? Dad wouldn't live forever, but he'd probably still be around. And Jay was already so totally different than he'd been. It would never be just like it had. Never. And Kevin wanted everything to stop.

Kevin snapped to and said, "Wait, back up, what did you just say?"

"A group of middle schoolers on Twitter," one of the other guys said. "Talking about blowing up the school. We investigated, and it wasn't a credible threat. But honestly, why would they even think of something like that?"

"It's a glamour thing," said his partner. "They read about school shootings and how the killer shoots himself afterward and then everyone raids their Facebook and Twitter feeds, and all their selfies get flashed across the news. It gives them something to look forward to."

"Dark," Kevin said.

"I'm glad I'm not growing up nowadays," Bill said.

"Yeah, but you're raising kids." One of the other officers shook his head. "And even if you raise yours right, you can't guarantee one of these maniacs isn't going to detonate in his presence."

Bill gave him a sarcastic smile. "Thanks. Thanks so much."

As Bill headed back to the store owner to talk to him about cleanup, Kevin said, "Sometimes, don't you just wish you could put the world back the way it should be? And keep it that way?"

"That's why we get the big bucks," said one of the other officers with a smirk. "And it's guaranteed full employment, because you know it's never going to work."

Kevin shivered. It wasn't cold, but he shivered.

On Monday after the morning Mass, Jay took the bus to St. Savior's Cathedral, diocesan headquarters, and with care he walked up the rain-glistening steps. He stayed a few minutes in the cathedral, then walked outside again to the main building. Wearing the priest uniform into such a grand office, peopled by so many others in the same uniform, he fought a smirk. *It's my new gang,* he prayed. Jay waited only five minutes before the bishop admitted him.

Bishop Sato's scrutinizing gaze landed on Jay like a wet newspaper, but Jay fought down the immediate nerves. "Thank you for seeing me, sir."

"You forget, I invited you. Please, sit." The bishop settled on the couch. "Don't look so nervous. It's not good for you." He took a deep breath, and under his studying gaze, Jay felt exposed.

Bishop Sato said, "How long has it been since you took time off?"

Fear spiked through Jay. "Who's been talking to you?"

The bishop started at Jay's reaction. "No one. You've got all the signs of burnout, and I can't afford to have any of my priests going to ground, especially not this soon out of seminary. You probably can't hear it in your own voice, but I've been hearing it for weeks. You're losing perspective. You've been working hard, and you need a break."

Jay could barely speak. "Who broke confidentiality?"

"Nobody," said the bishop. "But maybe there's something else you need to tell me?"

Doctor Lacks? No, it couldn't have been Dr. Lacks because Dr. Lacks hadn't known about the tingling or the blurriness until after he'd started playing phone-tag with the chancery. Maybe Father Jordan had called him out for not going to the graveside. Maybe Kevin wanted him "fired" from the priesthood. Maybe Gary had realized that morning when Jay's vision blacked out. Maybe. Maybe to all of them.

"I'm not quite sure what to think." The bishop sounded cautious. "What's going on?"

"It's not that bad," Jay said. "Whatever they told you."

"No one's told me anything," said Bishop Sato, "including you. So—tell me."

Jay explained softly, but hedging, what Dr. Lacks believed about the continuous stress.

The bishop stayed silent for a moment. Then, "You haven't had any vacation since your ordination, have you?"

Jay stared at his lap. "They need me."

"You're needed enough that I have to insist you save your strength." The bishop's voice was gentle, and those weren't the words you used to remove someone from a parish. "I need every priest I've got, but I really need *you.* We're losing three more this year to retirement, and we're only ordaining two."

Jay's hands tightened in his lap. He could do basic subtraction.

The bishop said, "You need some time off, and if your doctor's saying it too, then that's two of us. Do you have someplace you can stay?"

Swallowing, Jay shook his head.

"The Sisters of the Blessed Sacrament have a retreat house with a couple of rooms available for a visiting priest. It's a quiet environment, and it will do you good."

Do you good. Did he have to make it sound like a retirement home?

After a moment, Jay came out with, "Is that all?"

"In light of what you just told me, no." The bishop leaned back and folded his arms. "Give me a rough calculation of how much work you're doing."

Jay listed off the activities of a typical day, and the bishop seemed to approve of it all. The meetings, the counseling, the sacraments, the various groups, and of course the Caf. After Jay finished, the bishop said, "It's wonderful work, but it's at least ninety-five hours a week."

Jay shrugged.

"And it's never-ending. No wonder your health is going downhill."

Jay opened his hands. "Every priest does as much."

"I dispute your assumptions about your fellow priests—they work hard, but not to that extent. They're also not suffering stress-related illnesses. I want you to cut down to forty hours a week."

Jay's jaw dropped. "How?"

"Figure out your priorities in the parish and meet those needs first, then let the rest slide."

Jay's fists clenched. "I can't. They need me to—"

"Jay," the bishop said, "do you remember that vow of obedience?"

Jay recoiled.

"I don't like to overrule you that way, but if you must, think of it as a direct order. You are to immediately reduce your work week to forty hours. You're acting as if God Almighty can't keep the finance committee meeting on schedule without you. I assure you, He can." The bishop leveled his gaze on Jay. "Next item on the agenda, stop donating your salary back to the parish." When Jay protested, the bishop raised a hand. "It wasn't hard to figure out. I do look at the parish budgets, although I have to admit you were clever about hiding it."

Jay pursed his lips, wondering how the bishop would respond if he asked for three grand to pay for a funeral. He didn't, and the bishop continued, "God will find the money somehow."

Jay wore a deep scowl. "You're saying that from the diocesan seat, but it's not raining cash in the inner city parishes. The youth minister from Our Lady Queen of Angels needs to bury his mother, so he asked my parish for help. They don't have the money. We don't have it either, and we've got until three o'clock."

The bishop said, "His parish should be filing an emergency funding request."

Which would get processed in five weeks.

"There's an endless parade of needs that require money," said the bishop. "You can't fund them all.

You're a priest, but before that, you're a human being. You do have limits. You'll accomplish more if you're energetic and happy with your vocation."

Jay said flatly, "Yes, sir." After a hesitation, he added, "I'm sorry."

Something in his tone coaxed the bishop to study him momentarily.

"You're a good priest." The bishop stood from the couch and made his way back to his desk. "I'm remiss if you think you aren't. You're well worth the dispensations you needed to get ordained in the first place, and you've already surpassed my wildest expectations. I'm astonished by all you're accomplishing at St. Augustine's. Their last pastor is still bitter, but you turned the parish around. Your people love you."

Especially the drunk guys who interrupted Saturday night Mass. But Jay kept his arms folded and his chin down.

The bishop said, "Your name frequently comes up on the short list of candidates for the next bishop."

Jay's head shot up. "Don't do that to me!"

"Take this in the spirit I'm saying it, Jay: you don't stand a chance because you don't play politics." A smile softened the bishop's face. "I just think you ought to know I'm not the only one impressed. If you take it easier now, it'll be better in the long run. Pace yourself. Trust me."

In the lobby five minutes later, Jay crossed paths with Father Jordan of Saint Whatever's and said hello in a daze, then managed to get outside without having to speak to anyone else. He caught the crosstown bus from the steps of the cathedral.

Ordinarily he'd have prayed the rosary during the ride, but today an elderly woman changed seats to talk enthusiastically about St. Gus's after-Mass coffee hours, then followed up with an invitation to dinner with her family. Jay was relieved that when he got off the bus, she stayed.

The crosstown route left him a mile from St. Gus, and he wanted to walk the rest of the way despite the rain but just then the transfer bus pulled up. The driver hollered, "Hey, Father Jay, get in! We'll wait!"

He slowly climbed the steps. As Jay handed over the transfer, the driver barked at one of the kids in the first seats, "Get up! Can't you read?"

The seat had a sticker stating, "Please save these seats for the elderly or handicapped." Jay swallowed down his shame.

Unlike the crosstown, this bus was crowded. Its route ran directly through the three inner-city neighborhoods with the nickname "the Devil's Corridor," the last being his own. Someone in the back had a radio, and the interior had accumulated a general body odor.

A young woman pushed her way up to the front of the bus, and finally finding Jay, she beamed. "Father Jay! I'm so glad I saw you!"

Jay nodded. "You too, Linda."

"You'll never guess what happened!" She was grinning. "I got a real job! I'm an overnight accountant at the clinic downtown. It pays so much better than fast food, and I'll be able to stay home with Jocelyn."

Jay blinked. "That's good. Then your mother can watch her at night? But aren't you burning the candle at both ends?"

"It's only a few years. I couldn't stand to leave her in that daycare after all those violations." Linda smiled broadly. "She's so sweet, Father. Thanks."

Jay said, "Do you have a picture?"

Linda fiddled with her phone, then showed him a six-month-old wearing a bow in her silky fine hair. One year ago, a pregnant Linda had turned up at the rectory deserted by her boyfriend. She didn't want an abortion but thought she had no options. Jay had pounded on enough social service agencies that she could have the baby if she wanted, and she'd decided to. He'd also mediated between her and her mother so Linda could have a place to live while she finished high school. This was the result: a third shift accounting job, that chubby face on the screen, and a young woman who had pushed her way through the crowd to thank him for it.

Five minutes later, Jay walked into the rectory and went straight to his office. "Mrs. D, I need to talk to you now."

She followed, closing the door as he dropped into the chair behind his desk.

Her voice was beyond tense. "What's wrong?"

Jay directed his glare like a Las Vegas spotlight out the window. "I'm going to be gone the rest of the week."

He gave the briefest explanation possible. She sat looking serious, saying nothing until he finished.

Mrs. D said, "I'll handle everything."

Jay stared through her in exhaustion.

"I've worked here for three other pastors. I know what needs to be done."

Jay cast his gaze at his lap.

She added, "For what it's worth, I've been worried about you too."

She slipped out of his office, closing the door again at her back.

Jay pulled out the retreat house phone number and sat looking at the paper for five minutes before picking up the phone and dialing a completely different number. Father Ron, his spiritual advisor.

After listening to Jay's entire monologue, Father Ron agreed with Dr. Lacks and the bishop.

Jay said, "What should I do?" His voice surprised him by holding steady. There was a knock at his door. He ignored it.

Father Ron said, "Relax for a week. It's not like you have a choice about the hours. Satan would love to derail your ministry, and he doesn't care if you derail it with sloth or you derail it with overwork."

Jay said, "Or I could just, you know, work."

"And you could just, you know, burn out. What was the first thing Father Martin said when you took over St. Gus? 'Sure you look happy now, but watch out for the hyenas.'"

Jay sighed. "Close enough." Someone knocked again, and Jay swiveled his chair so he faced the back wall.

Father Ron was saying, "Do what you'd tell a married couple to do: remember why you fell in love. Try to remember what it was that attracted you to the vocation."

"I'm not falling out of love with the priesthood. There's just so much to do. The parish—"

"No, no, Jay. You're like a neurotic new mother who comes in saying her baby needs her so much she can't even take a shower." As Jay smirked, Father Ron continued, "Keep some perspective. Set your priorities."

"Speaking of priorities, you wouldn't happen to have three grand, would you?"

Father Ron laughed. "Oh, you're going to serve steak at the Caf?"

"Hardly. The youth minister at OLQA needs to bury his mother."

"Oh, dear." Father Ron let off a long breath. "No, I don't. I'll think about who else you can ask."

"Think fast," Jay said. "If I don't have it by three this afternoon, my boys plan to steal a car."

Father Ron got off the phone, and Jay returned to the front office.

As soon as he walked in, he found Mrs. D staring with tearful eyes. "Father Jay," she whispered.

And he knew right then: God had come through. Somehow, either they didn't need the money any longer or else they had it right here in the office.

She whispered, "We have the money."

Jay felt the smile unfurl in a way he couldn't contain. "How?"

"It's an extremely anonymous donation." Mrs. D clutched the check. "I've been sworn to secrecy."

Jay reached for the check, but Mrs. D pulled it back beyond arm's reach. "It won't do you any good anyhow. It's a bank check. Just an account number."

"You're cruel." Jay folded his arms. "Who was it?"

"I don't know. Someone walked into this office and handed me a check. I said, 'You know, we've already spent it,' and the person replied, 'I'm sure you have.'"

Jay lowered himself into the chair by Mrs. D's desk.

"Exactly three thousand," she said.

God— He didn't even have the words. Trying to come up with a thank-you, he kept finding nothing at all.

Mrs. D was saying, "We won't even have to wait for it to clear."

Jay said, "And now you've got to—"

"Already filled out the deposit slip. I'm off!"

Jay said, "Speed all the way to the bank. Maybe God will get you out of a traffic ticket too."

She laughed as she departed.

The office settled into quiet, at least until the music upstairs started again. He ought to send the boys a group text telling them to knock it off, but it wasn't a battle he felt like fighting right now.

Instead Jay headed to the church and unbolted the door, then locked it again behind himself.

On the side table, waiting for tomorrow's Mass, were the new chalice and paten given by Father Jordan. They gleamed, brand new and yet cast off by another parish, whereas his needed everything.

He couldn't provide for his congregation. They kept having to rely on everyone else.

Kneeling in the benches before the tabernacle, Jay started the rosary. He didn't get further than the second mystery before he realized he had no idea where he was in the prayer.

Staring at the beads, he huddled forward against the back of the next bench. "I'm sorry," he whispered, then said it again as tears started to come. A grief as real as the death of his parents, as the death of the his old reckless and healthy self: he let go and sobbed, hating the way he couldn't stop, his rosary crunched in his hands, his shoulders and arms tight like steel cables. "I just couldn't keep going. I failed you again."

What a useless, useless crybaby—couldn't do a darned thing for anyone. Jay made his way to the sacristy and pulled a handful of tissues from the box, then stood with his hands over his eyes, gasping. He'd only been a priest three years. It was all dissolving so fast.

Eight

Jay still looked like death, and that was the nicest thing Kevin could say about him when he walked in the door with Holly. At the funeral he'd looked bad, but what stared back at Kevin now went beyond exhaustion and well into defeat.

Holly kissed Kevin. "It smells great in here!"

Kevin said to Jay, "Did she drag you behind the car, or is this some kind of priest chic?"

"Kevin!" she exclaimed, but Jay only replied, "Priest chic. Maybe I'll start a trend."

"Have you slept at all since last Friday?" Kevin led the way into his apartment's eat-in kitchen, the source of the smells that had made Holly so happy. "If your homeless Archangels are keeping you awake playing music all night, I'll have a patrol visit them to discuss the concept of the noise violation."

"They're fine." Jay looked over the pots on the stovetop. "What have we got here? And where did you learn to cook?"

"YouTube," Kevin said.

Holly laughed. "I certainly didn't teach him."

Jay said, "I got a large print edition of *Cooking for the Barely Competent*, and now I can heat soup and microwave a pizza."

Kevin said, "I got my Advanced Beginner badge in jar opening. I can boil pasta too."

Jay sat at the kitchen table, then said, "Oh, I'm sorry, did you want us to wait in the living room and get out of your way?"

Kevin laughed out loud. "Where'd that come from? Did they give you manners when they gave you a parish?"

Holly started setting the table, and Jay leaned back. Kevin knew he was talking too loud and joking too much, but Jay—Jay looked like an old man even though he was only a year older than Kevin, not in his sixties. "Do your parishioners tithe with home-cooked meals?"

"They do, actually. It's kind of funny." Jay forced a smile. "Remember how we used to end up at everyone else's house near lunch or dinner, and we'd stay just in case we could nab a meal that way?"

Holly said, "Really?"

Kevin nodded. "The guys at the station laugh because I'll eat anything, but when we lived with Dad, mooching was a life skill."

Jay said, "Remember Harlan? He'd call in to Stardust Pizza with a pickup order like a large pie with jalapeño, anchovies, and pineapples, and we'd wait in the alley. Half an hour later, they'd throw it in the dumpster because obviously no one else would want it, and then Harlan would drag the thing out of the trash. That would be dinner."

Holly looked horrified. "Really?"

Kevin added, "Nothing the other cops have ever suggested has quite equalled Harlan's combos."

"I don't know if the boys upstairs do stunts like that." Jay sounded mildly amused. "I'm not sure how to ask without giving them ideas."

"Fortunately," Kevin said as he set a colander in the sink, "we're not quite that free-range tonight."

"Darn," Jay murmured. "I was looking forward to canned peaches and sardines."

"Next time." Kevin drained the pasta, then mixed in the sauce. A few minutes later, he had everything on the table (a little close, but not uncomfortably so) and Holly was ladling out pasta for everyone.

"So these," Kevin said with flourish, "are called *strozzapreti*. Priest-stranglers!"

Holly laughed. "Really?"

"Absolutely. I answered a call at an Italian market where they sell fresh pasta, and they had this listed on the wall."

Jay forced a smile. "Does that make you their hired assassin?"

Kevin said, "The statutes aren't entirely clear, but since I paid them for the privilege, it's just me killing you for fun, not part of an exchange."

Holly said, "That's a relief. They're in the clear, so I can still get my lasagna noodles." She turned to Jay. "Will you say grace?"

Kevin tensed. Jay glanced at him nervously, then bowed his head and said something about food and thankfulness that lasted about ten seconds. Then they dug in, and the banter resumed.

Jay still didn't look good, but the food gave him some energy. Maybe in addition to not sleeping enough, he wasn't eating enough. Maybe something awful had just happened.

Jay told them about the black cat. "The boys say they're not bringing it inside," Jay said.

Kevin raised his soda glass in a toast. "Congratulations on your new cat!"

Jay shook his head. "I don't need a cat. If I keep putting it out, eventually it should go somewhere else."

"Cats don't work that way. You're now officially owned." Holly laughed. "And I see you got married."

Shyly, Jay held up his left hand for Kevin to see a slender gold band on the fourth finger.

Wedding ring? Mom's wedding ring?

"Nuns always got to wear wedding rings," Jay said to Holly. "Now they're encouraging priests. It's my mother's. One of my parishioners works in a jewelry store and sized it." Jay's brows furrowed. "Then he wouldn't take any money."

Yes, Mom's wedding ring. And then he'd told Dad to send out the diamond. Jerk.

Holly shrugged. "They size any ring you buy. No big deal."

Jay shook his head. "There was a price posted. I don't know why he didn't charge it."

Kevin was fuming. "Because it's you. People think God will take care of them if they pander to you."

Jay winced. "I'd like to think they have loftier motives."

"That's the difference between you and me," Kevin said. It wasn't the time to have it out with Jay about the ring now, with Holly here. Not unless he mentioned it in front of her. "I gave up on people doing the right thing long ago. Speaking of which, did Richard Cantrel's parents ever call about the kid?"

A sudden ferocity shadowed Jay's face. "Seth's grandmother called the rectory and then refused to speak to me. No, she has a thousand reasons why she can't handle this. It's so difficult...he reminds her of her son...it's too much...she can't get out of bed...and on and on and on. If he's not there, she can pretend her son is still alive. The woman kept Mrs. D on the phone half an hour and it was all about herself."

Holly said, "She did just lose her son."

"Her *grandson* just lost his *father*," Jay said, "and I should think that takes precedence no matter how you do the math. But don't worry, he'll be *much better off with us* because *they don't have WiFi*."

Holly said, "Did they offer to reimburse you for his housing, like you're a hotel?"

"Oh my goodness." Jay's cheeks went grey. "I bet you they did. We just got a huge anonymous donation."

Kevin huffed. "Welcome to capitalism. Don't want your grandson? Pay someone else to raise him."

Jay's shoulders fell. "I don't even have the option of giving it back."

"Keep it," said Holly. "You end up better off in both directions: St. Gus gets the money *and* the kid, who's far more of a treasure than his grandparents ever were."

Kevin side-eyed her. "That's the kind of comment I'd expect from me."

She winked. "You're rubbing off."

Everyone fell silent for a moment, and Kevin wondered again why Jay was so drawn, but he couldn't come up with anything to say other than to ask what Jay thought of his priest-stranglers. The pasta was a weird shape, a long sheet curled in an S-curve along its axis. Jay nodded and said they were the best-tasting murder weapon he'd ever faced.

And there ended that conversation.

Holly said, "Oh, do you mind if I pump you for a theological gotcha?"

Jay shrugged.

"One of the new waitresses has made it her personal mission to convert me to her branch of Christianity."

Kevin said, "Convert you? You're already Christian."

"Not according to her." Holly rolled her eyes. "I'm an idol-worshipping, Pope-revering rosary-slinger who believes she can work her way into Heaven."

Kevin frowned. "Isn't hard work a good thing?"

Jay said, "Count yourself lucky you haven't been exposed to this nonsense." He sighed. "Protestant denominations hold to *sola fide,* meaning only faith gets you into Heaven, but some have spun that out to the point where they think any mention of hard work is evil."

Holly touched Kevin's hand. "The Bible says faith alone without love is about as useful as a clashing cymbal, and I told her Galatians 5:6 says it's *faith working in love,* but she doesn't care what the Bible says. And I'm not the one who started the fight."

Jay looked weary. "It's just a tribal differentiation thing. The more reactionary Protestants have decided that since they believe in *sola fide,* and Catholics are by definition evil, then that must mean Catholics believe you can work your way into Heaven. But I've never, not once, met a Catholic who thought you could work your way into Heaven."

"I realize it's a straw man argument," Holly said, "but I get attacked by her straw man every day. Every time I mention anything, or even if I haven't, it's always, *Surely you aren't implying your works matter!* That's why I need a gotcha line for when she tries to jack-in-the-box me."

Jay shook his head. "She's not interested in debate."

Holly nodded. "So help me stop her cold."

"She won't listen to you because she's not even listening to herself," Jay said. "As soon as she complains about your supposed emphasis on *works*, she's emphasizing how much *she herself* values works—or rather, values not doing them. Because if all that mattered was faith, and you've got faith, then who cares if you think God likes it when you do something good?" He laughed, and that was the first time all night Kevin had heard him sounding relaxed. It figured he'd only relax when he turned to God-talk. "If she were right, even if you thought your good works could get you into Heaven, your faith would do it anyhow."

Holly blinked. "Oh!"

"What she's saying instead is she believes that good works are capable of keeping you *out* of Heaven...which is exactly what she objects to you thinking."

Holly laughed out loud. "Catch-22!"

"And if 'acts of service' is a love language," Jay added, "then how dare anyone tell you that you aren't allowed to express your love of God? She's jack-hammering a very narrow-minded viewpoint into your relationship with your own Creator, and that's not cool. Particularly since she's probably going to insist that a person's relationship with God is the most important part."

Holly smirked. "Can I just keep a mini *Jay Farrell* in my pocket?"

"Just pray for her." Jay looked annoyed. "She's wrapped around the axel about Catholicism for reasons she doesn't understand and most of which aren't true. Live out your faith and let God deal with her."

Everyone got quiet again, and Kevin couldn't take it anymore. "Okay, spit it out. What's wrong?"

Jay looked up, surprised.

"You look down," Holly said.

"Down? You look dejected. What's going on?"

Jay twisted his napkin. "Everything. The bishop wants me put out to pasture."

Holly gasped. "You're being moved?"

"I'm staying at St. Gus, but he wants me in a retreat house for a week." Jay stopped eating, and Kevin studied his body language: it was all wrong. Jay shouldn't be resigned like this. Jay was a fighter. "All the old injuries are acting up. My vision is deteriorating, and I'm getting migraines. The doctor thinks it's stress, and the bishop ordered me to stand down. Effective now."

Holly sounded tentative. "What does that mean?"

"I have to cut back my hours to forty a week," Jay said.

Kevin choked. "That's not exactly putting you out to pasture."

Jay looked murderous. "I have work to do. I don't spend my days on a throne ordering my servants to fetch me a coffee. And for the next week he wants me to retire to this retreat house run by the sweetest order of nuns. I know who goes there. It's all priests over a hundred years old, and the nuns baby them like they're wrapped in cotton balls."

Kevin smirked. "Old man."

Jay's eyebrows shot up. "I'm not that old."

"Maybe you can get a flight down to Dad's condo community and have all those little old ladies fuss over you instead."

Jay rolled his eyes. "Not an improvement, Kevin."

Kevin said, "But why do you need to go to the old age home?"

"Bishop Sato was trying hard to sell it to me, too. It'll be soothing, relaxing...I can spend the whole day praying." Jay blew off a breath. "No, thank you."

Kevin frowned. "I can scour the airfares. We can find something cheap and send you to Dad. I mean, I was joking about the little old ladies, but the complex has a pool, and Dad orders the best take-out."

Jay gave a quirky smile. "I appreciate it, but you have no idea how much I have to do. I can't go to Florida, even if I could afford it."

Kevin said, "Then stay with me"

It slipped out so quickly he hadn't even thought about it, and his mouth rushed to catch up to the offer he'd just made. "This complex has a gym associated with it, so you could go during the daytime. We don't have nuns to fuss over you. When I'm at work, you just lock the door and everyone leaves you alone."

Holly brightened. "That's actually not a bad idea."

Jay looked doubtful. "You don't have any room here."

Holly said, "I can borrow an air mattress."

That Jay had already considered it for fifteen seconds left Kevin stunned: was the situation that dire?

Jay mused, "You're not far from the bus line. I could get back in to St. Gus a couple of times."

This had gone from zero to sixty very quickly. Kevin said, "When was the last time we lived in the same house?"

Jay frowned. "Before I enlisted, probably."

"And a bit after you came home from the hospital," Kevin said.

"And then Dad kicked me out into a rehab place." Jay shook his head. "He was terrified I wouldn't be able to live on my own and he'd have to take care of me for the rest of my life. And look," Jay said, opening his hands, "he wasn't wrong!"

"Please," Holly said. "The doctor and the bishop are talking about taking *one week off* and *working forty-hour weeks*. That's what most people call *life*."

Jay didn't look convinced.

Kevin tried to sound breezy. "Well, you know my hours. You might get woken up when I come in late. And there's not much space."

Jay's voice ticked down. "It's okay. I can go stay with the nuns."

Kevin shook his head. "No, no." This conversation kept going in ways he didn't plan it to, and he wasn't even sure anymore what outcome he was aiming for. He just wanted Jay to quit looking like someone had stuck a Shop-Vac into his spirit and suctioned out all the insides.

The thing about Jay, the thing Kevin clung to as a pillar, was that Jay never gave up. You took something from him, no matter how vital, and he just dusted himself off and said, "Okay, so we can't do that. What can we do?" and did that instead. Okay, we don't have a mom anymore and our dad vanished, but we have each other. Okay, we don't have a family, but we can have a gang. Okay, we don't have a future, but we can have right now. On and on and on. And finally, it had been, okay, so I don't have my sight and I don't have my balance and I can't do anything I ever wanted to do before: so what can I do?

Of course, then Jay had gone for the Big Fairy Tale, but at least he'd done something.

Sending Jay to the nuns felt like saying, *You can't do anything.* If Kevin could give it back to him, the chance to think he had a purpose, he'd sleep on the floor for a week and make space for another toothbrush. He'd just have to deal with how they annoyed the heck out of each other when they were in close quarters for too long. You couldn't really understate that. But the police department made you flexible about tradeoffs. Once Jay started annoying him, it probably meant Jay was on the mend.

So Kevin said, "You stay here. You tell the nuns thanks, but no thanks. I'll figure out how to get in and out without waking you up, and you get the pass code for the gym."

Jay looked brilliantly sulky. "I know how to adjust my sleep schedule, you know."

Holly said, "I'll get that air mattress, so it'll only be tonight on the couch."

Jay shook his head. "I need to go home and tie things up." He focused his narrow gaze right into Kevin's eyes. "Thank you. I appreciate it."

It wasn't Jay. There wasn't any fire. Kevin's heart fell.

Nine

Kevin, even though he could have let Holly drive Jay back, insisted on driving Jay home himself. And that was a bad sign. It meant Kevin wanted to *talk*.

Even worse, he hadn't wanted to talk in front of Holly.

Again in the passenger seat, an eternal condition due to those pesky regulations about driving while legally blind, Jay waited. And waited. Kevin had a few details for him about the logistics of bunking together, but only deeply emotional topics like, "You okay with corn flakes?"

They drove another silent mile until Kevin said, "I never really apologized to you for staying away all those years. I just returned, and you took me back without question."

Jay swiveled to look out the side window. He didn't want to hear this now. But maybe it was like an organized crime lord's confession; maybe Kevin needed to say it. So Jay didn't prompt him to continue, but he didn't derail him either.

When Jay gave no response, Kevin said, "When I saw how much you were doing for your people there at the church, and how much you meant to them, the least I should have done was be willing to call you my brother. They were willing to die for you, and I didn't even want to talk to you. I was being a total heel, and you were probably praying for me."

Jay laughed darkly. "I'm not that holy. Every time I'd try to pray for you, I'd start saying things like, 'And God, make that idiot come to his senses,' and I'd have to stop."

Kevin laughed out loud. "Really?"

Jay waited to see if that completed tonight's agenda. "Is the health thing really that bad?"

Okay, slightly more sensitive subject. This might be it. "Dr. Lacks said if I don't take time off, in six months I'll be totally blind."

Kevin sat up straighter in the driver's seat. "No kidding?"

"A few months beyond that, I'll be test-driving the leading brand of wheelchair."

Kevin's eyes shone against his pale cheeks. "You're sure he wasn't trying to scare you?"

"He succeeded. I suspected as much, though. My eyes have been flaking out on me lately."

"You look like the undead, too." Kevin hummed. "So why not do what they say and take it easy for a while?"

Jay's eyes lowered. "I don't really have a choice. Not that I like it. But I'm under orders."

Kevin choked back a "Hah!"

Jay said, "Look, I know I was never exactly obedient with Dad, but it's different now. I made a promise to God to obey, and you shouldn't break those promises."

"All that aside, I don't see why you need to be under orders. Taking it easy is the sensible thing to do."

"I'm an old man now." Jay sighed. "I have to do the sensible thing."

Kevin sounded unamused. "Working yourself to death is actually not a terrific plan."

Jay turned his head. "When you came to St. Gus the first time, you accused me of running away to find a cushy life for myself. That's exactly what I'll have."

Kevin slapped a hand into the dashboard. "For crying out loud, Jay, when did you ever start listening to me?"

In a low voice, Jay said, "I always listened to you. Even when I didn't agree."

"So you pick now to start agreeing?" Kevin shook his head. "No one would see this as anything other than saving your life."

"At what cost? Who pays the price for my surviving yet again?"

"The diocese," Kevin said. "They keep writing you checks and you keep cashing them, and every so often you get to be everyone's hero."

"Maybe heroics start with self-discipline." He turned aside and stared directly away from Kevin, squinting hard through the glasses and finally putting his hand to his eyes. "But maybe it's time for a different sort of heroism, the kind where you accept where you are. I've wrecked my life often enough. It's time for someone else to get a turn."

Kevin said, "Speaking of wrecking our lives, do you realize that when you asked Dad for Mom's wedding ring, he turned right around and sent me her engagement ring too?"

And on that angry note, Jay recognized the real intent of the conversation. As if this were a police interrogation, everything else had been the warm-up.

"Well?"

"Is that why you apologized to me, as prepayment for confidences received?" Jay glowered through the floor of the car, as if he could see the road passing under their tires. "I suggested that. It's not like I'm going to wear it, and it's probably worth more, so you got the better end of the bargain."

"Didn't you even think this through?" Kevin exclaimed. "He sent me an engagement ring—with the expectation that I'm supposed to get engaged with it."

Kevin's voice had picked up enough frustration that Jay said, "I don't care what you do with Mom's ring. Sell it on eBay. Give it to the grocery store in exchange for fifty boxes of generic corn flakes. It's none of my business."

"It shouldn't have been your business from the start!"

Jay said, "Why are you arguing with me over something that takes up no space and you don't have to use and you didn't have to pay for?"

"Because," Kevin snapped, "it's intrusive."

"Sorry. There was an extra ring lying around and I thought, maybe someday my brother will want to get married, and—"

"And I don't," Kevin said.

Jay let it sit. They both agreed it was none of his business.

Kevin said, "In your rectory right now, don't you have a kid whose parents were shot right in his house because his father was a cop?"

Jay furrowed his brow. "See, now, I thought this was none of my business."

"Not when you're shoving an engagement down my throat."

This wasn't a police interrogation. This was more like a combat confessional. What was going on here? "Stay single if you want. But don't go planning your whole life as a rebellion against a piece of jewelry."

"I'm not your parishioner," Kevin snapped. "I don't need a sermon."

"You're my brother," Jay shot back, "and not every suggestion is a sermon."

"Being my brother doesn't give you an excuse to run my life. It's not like you've done such a great job running your own."

Jay bit back an, "I already said that!" and instead clenched his fist in his lap. Jaw tight, he stared straight ahead at the blurry headlights in the oncoming traffic.

This wasn't about an engagement ring. Kevin had started the conversation by saying something...what had it been?...about Jay holding back information...but Kevin was holding back something too. *A kid whose parents were shot right in his house.* Was that it? Was he upset that the police weren't taking care of their own?

Or was Kevin just afraid to die? And now he had Jay sitting in the passenger seat, dying by pieces right before his eyes?

It made no sense, so Jay kept his mouth shut to avoid escalating an argument he didn't understand. Kevin had him trapped, so he'd just ride it through to the end. Life had treated Jay this way often enough.

With Kevin strangling the wheel, they sat at a red light, then rolled forward through the green while Jay grappled for anything to say. Finally he came up with, "I'm sorry I inadvertently started this. I wanted Mom's ring, and I didn't want to be unfair, so I suggested the split. I didn't consider the emotional baggage."

And here he stopped.

Glaring straight forward, Kevin said, "Isn't emotional baggage part of your job?"

"I'm not very good at my job."

Kevin choked out a surprised laugh.

Jay tried to sound breezy. "Mom's ring wouldn't look good on you anyway."

Kevin still sounded bitter. "And it's too small."

"I know a guy who resizes rings."

Kevin said, "And after he resizes the ring, then what? He dies too?"

Oh! "The ring isn't a death omen."

Kevin huffed. "Your health fell apart right after you started wearing it."

Jay paused. "Are you saying they're cursed? And you claim *I* believe the unbelievable?" He looked at Kevin. "No, I get it. It's bad luck to begin something with a symbolic object that's available only because something else ended."

Kevin's nose wrinkled. "What? Did they teach you that kind of stuff in seminary?"

"What I love most about you," Jay said, "is that your agnosticism is completely, one-hundred-percent honest agnosticism. You don't know about God, but you admit it's possible. You don't know about curses or omens, but you admit they're possible. So in your mind, it's equally possible that God does exist as that God doesn't exist, and the same with curses. But I think we can rule out some things. The engagement diamond didn't absorb Mom's bad luck, and neither of us is going to get hit by a drunk driver just because it's in your possession."

Kevin said, "I still don't want to get married."

"None of my business," Jay said.

When they reached the rectory, Jay said, "I assume I should call the nuns to make new arrangements for the rest of the week."

"I'll come get you tomorrow." Kevin sounded like he was done with the anger, although Jay remained shaken. Kevin never let go of anything that quickly. "I'll get you a copy of the key and the gym pass, and you can be moved in before I go to work."

Inside the rectory, Jay found Seth at the front door exhausted and unsteady. It was only nine o'clock. Noises upstairs told Jay the boys were still awake (of course they were) so he asked Seth to come up with him, and he gathered everyone in the tiny kitchen.

"Everyone" tonight was only three: Seth, Esai, and an older kid Jay had seen once a couple of months ago. Eric, he thought. "I'm leaving for a week because I'm not feeling well," he said.

"Do we gotta leave?" asked Esai.

"You can stay here if you don't trash the place, but I'll be locking my apartment. I'll probably come back from time to time," Jay added.

The older kid said, "Are you going to die?"

"Not going to die." Jay glanced at Seth, who had absolutely no facial expression. "But I have to work less for a while. Eat right, sleep late, and get some exercise."

Esai said, "Because you're crippled?"

Seth exclaimed, "You can't say that!"

Esai shrugged. "But he is."

Jay forced a confident tone. "My doctor said to take time off so these things don't get worse."

Seth said, "Will the Church take you away from here?"

Jay swallowed. "I hope not."

"I'll follow you," Seth said. "Wherever you go, I'm going there too."

Ten

Jay woke up to footsteps overhead. Woke up like a shot, heart pounding.

Instinct moved him at times like this, instinct or the Holy Spirit—he was happy to credit either one. He slipped out of bed and made his way upstairs as quietly as possible.

The rectory had been robbed a few times (one of the reasons he didn't have a television) and he would willingly let the diocese's insurance company take the fall except for those guests on the top floor.

At the top, he flung open the basement door and called, "Who's there?"

A startled gasp, and then, "Oh. Oh, it's you. I'm sorry, Father."

Jay groped for the light switch, which momentarily revealed Seth, breath heaving, pressed to the wall.

Jay's voice was raspy. "What's going on?"

"I think someone's in the building." Seth's voice barely reached Jay's ears. "I heard something."

Jay knew exactly what was going on. He'd felt the same twenty years ago, and his mother hadn't even died in the house. "Let's look."

Seth stayed behind Jay as they walked through the corridor, as if Jay could fend off an intruder and save both their lives.

"The cat's back," Seth said. "Maybe that's what I heard."

Jay frowned. "I wish that thing would go away."

Seth said, "How's it getting in?"

"Probably one of the screens is loose." The rectory had settled enough during the last century that f you opened a bag of marbles, they'd all roll into one of the corners. With no right angles, nothing sat quite right in its frame.

At the front of the house, Jay opened the door. Normal enough: street lights, most windows black, the cars nothing but shapes in the darkness. He felt confident in pronouncing the rectory intruder-free.

"It's so big, though." Seth shivered. "Maybe someone's hiding."

While brisk, the night wasn't chilly, and Seth was wearing street clothes rather than pajamas, so Jay sat on the steps.

Seth leaned against the porch post, arms folded and staring at the steps. He seemed so much older than twelve, so much angrier. Had Jay looked like that after his mother's death? Kevin hadn't. Probably. There weren't many photos of them after Mom died because Mom had been the one taking pictures. There hadn't, for that matter, been many pictures of her, and it limited what they had to remember her by.

Seth looked up. "It's so dark without the moon."

Jay rubbed his mother's wedding ring. "Do you have any pictures of your parents?"

Seth took the phone out of his pocket as though it were one of those new fancy phones that weighed forty thousand pounds, and he scrolled until he flashed the screen at Jay. He and his mother had been at a gun range, decked out with protective gear and first using a Glock 22, then an AR-15. Seth looked so much younger, but it was on his phone, so how long ago could it possibly have been?

"I'm sorry," Jay said. "I wish I could make it right."

"Masa said your mother died too." Seth clenched his teeth. "It's not fair."

Jay said, "It's only been eight days for you."

"Not even. It's Monday, right? It's a week. Oh, gosh." Seth sounded baffled. "How could it only be a week?"

Jay said, "One week straight out of hell."

Seth shuddered. "It was *Monday*. I mean, what happens on Mondays? I had baseball practice."

Jay said, "What position do you play?"

"Shortstop. But Esai's teaching me to play basketball. He says I don't suck as bad as I did when I got here."

"That's high praise." Jay chuckled. "The parish thought I was nuts for installing a basketball court, but the previous pastor had left a line item in the budget for capital improvements, so now we have a basketball team. I taught them to shoot free throws, and they taught me to trash talk."

Seth said, "I don't get you."

"I don't get you either." That was kind of a lie, but Jay hoped God wouldn't hold it against him. "You could be in an air-conditioned private bedroom with a security system and a grocery delivery service."

"My grandparents are jerks." Seth hunched forward. "They hate me. They hated my mom."

Jay swallowed hard. "That's a shame. They probably feel bad about that now."

"You didn't hear Granddad going off about her after the funeral, like it's a shame my parents got buried together. And Grandmom can't stand to look at me. I look too much like Dad. She sees me and bursts into tears, so eventually she just locked herself in her bedroom and made Granddad bring her food."

Flames rose inside Jay's heart.

Seth said, "So I left. I didn't know you let kids live here. But I knew where you were because Father Jordan told me."

Jay's eyes widened. "He knew you were running away?"

Seth laughed out loud. "No! But you were the only person at the whole stupid funeral who cared about the fact that my parents were dead. Everyone else wanted to *pay their respects* or honor the police force or thank my grandparents for their sacrifice or some stupid nonsense. So I asked Father Jordan for your address and said I wanted to write you a thank you note."

Jay hadn't said anything incredible or imposing at the funeral. What had he said at all? He'd spoken to Seth in the receiving line. He'd prayed for him at the prayer of the faithful. But maybe to a soul all alone, hemorrhaging and in need, that was all it took. The only thing that mattered, really, was that Seth needed help, and God had put them together.

Seth said, "Anyhow, it took like all morning to bike over here, and Esai was on the porch and said, 'Oh, you moving in?' and I said yes. I didn't know you did this on a regular basis, but I think it's cool. Father Jordan never did anything like that."

Father Jordan probably hadn't gotten into quite as much trouble with the bishop, either. Jay said, "Our parishes have different needs."

Seth said, "That sounds an awful lot like, *Father Jordan isn't anywhere near as cool.*"

Jay murmured, "Please don't tell him I said anything of the sort."

Seth laughed out loud.

"Could you go live with your mother's parents?"

Seth said, "I doubt it. They're a lot older, and they live a thousand miles away."

"Do you have any cousins?"

Seth shrugged. "I don't think they want me."

And I think I want their phone number. Jay said, "Well, you can stay as long as you need, but it's best if you're living somewhere stable."

"Masa said I can go to school with him."

Oh, the Catholic middle school administration would be five colors of pleased when they heard that. They already gave full scholarships to two of the Archangels. Plus, Masa had recruited from their regular students to form a branch of the Archangels to take care of the school. On the other hand, Jay was already one of their least favorite people, so how much worse could it get? Time to find out.

Seth said, "You're being really cool about this."

Jay said, "Did you know I was your age when my mother died?"

Seth's head picked up. "How?"

"Car crash. Drunk driver. My brother and I lived with my father afterward, but we might as well have been on our own. He brought in a paycheck and worked a lot of overtime and let us run wild. I don't know if it's because we reminded him of Mom or just because it's awful to lose your wife."

Seth was totally silent. Jay picked his words carefully. "My brother and I needed a family. We went after it the wrong way, and we joined a gang. It was as close to family as we were going to get, and it was an awful mistake. I dragged my brother into it, and I regret that."

Seth said, "Did the gang shoot you up and that's why you're sick?"

Jay said, "That happened in the army. I drove over a land mine in Iraq."

Seth gasped. "So you nearly died just the way your mom did!"

Jay hadn't framed it that way, and he shivered. It had nothing to do with the night's temperature. He twisted the ring on his finger, reminding himself it wasn't a cursed object. "No one's going to break in and kill you."

"I was upstairs when that monster came in." Seth's voice grew shrill. "I was right upstairs, but I was playing SpaceJunk and I didn't go down when I heard the door open."

Jay put a hand on Seth's shoulder. "It wouldn't have helped."

"I know how to shoot," Seth said. "I could have shot him!"

Jay said, "It's easy to shoot, but killing?"

"To save my mom—of course I would!"

Jay pulled Seth toward him, and Seth buried his face in Jay's shoulder. "Your mom wouldn't have wanted you involved. Your dad would have told you to stay upstairs. They'd have rather saved you than have you risk your life or live a lifetime knowing you killed someone. You know that."

"You don't know that." Seth's fists clenched into his shoulders. "I could have shot that monster in the face. I heard gunshots, and I hid in my closet. They're dead because of me."

Jay held him tighter. "They're dead because a man with a gun did something evil. You couldn't have stopped him."

Seth's muscles were tight like iron. He wasn't going to fight, but he didn't agree. He'd just keep his personal guilt locked close to his heart and never let anyone know.

Jay said, "I wasn't even in the car with my mother, and I blamed myself. We do that because grieving is awful, not because it's true."

It was too late. Seth had tuned him out, and Jay knew better than to try getting back his attention. So instead he said, "No one's going to break into the rectory. You can go back to sleep. The Archangels claimed us as their own, and everyone around here knows it."

Seth pulled away. He hadn't been crying. Instead he walked back inside without meeting Jay's eyes, and Jay listened until Seth shut one of the upstairs doors and the last glimmer of light went out.

Then the house remained quiet except for the car crash Jay could still hear in his mind.

Eleven

It never failed to surprise Kevin that there were cars parked in the church lot. No matter when he came, there were always two or three, clustered near the rectory or near the church door, and they were always different.

People, then, drifting in and out. Taking care of business or slipping away for some peace and quiet.

They came here to relax, right, so why was Jay so stressed? Or did they give their stress to Jay like a religious offering? Pass the plate, pass your issues off to some victim, and then go home secure because someone else was going to take care of it all?

Although (and here Kevin had to chuckle) they did that to the police too. *Father, go chat up God and tell him I need a job. Officer, go chat up my tenant and tell him I need him to turn down the stereo.*

Kevin walked up the rectory steps through the pattering rain and entered a building whose smell had become familiar by now. Not a mildew smell, but more like institutionalized dust and human use. It smelled of age.

He found Mrs. D looking efficient as ever behind her desk, and Jay came out of his office. "What still needs to be done?"

"Everything fell into place," Mrs. D said. "I've canceled all your evening meetings and rescheduled most of your regular appointments. The rest I'm waiting for calls back. The Cure d'Ars House has priests available to take all the daily Masses except Wednesday."

Jay turned to Kevin. "Cure d'Ars House is the retirement center for diocesan priests. Did I say I was being put out to pasture? No, I'm being *replaced* by priests who were put out to pasture."

Kevin smirked. "Even better."

Mrs. D continued, "Wednesday may end up being a Communion service instead."

Jay muttered, "Gary's going to have a liturgical fit."

Mrs. D grinned. "I can handle Gary. And one of the priests will handle confessions, so you don't need to come back until Saturday at five."

Jay shook his head. "Youth group."

Behind Kevin came a voice. "I'll run it."

Kevin pivoted, and Jay rushed past him toward a rain-dotted man standing meekly in the doorway. The newcomer tried to shake Jay's hand and ended up hugging him instead, getting rain all over Jay in the process.

Jay said, "I'm so sorry. I wish it wasn't something awful that brought you back here again." He turned to Kevin. "This is Enrique Hoyos. We worked together at my former parish. Enrique, this is my brother."

Enrique shook Kevin's hand, not hiding how he looked him over.

Mrs. D approached with an envelope. Enrique swallowed as he took it. "Thanks so much for helping. I know you don't have the money any more than OLQA does."

Jay shrugged. "God had it."

"And now I've got you. I'll take the youth group." He offered a smile. "I came by to say thank you before you left, but if you need me, that's great. I can't say Mass or hear Confessions, but I can handle the kids."

Jay frowned. "They're a tough group."

Enrique raised his eyebrows. "Tougher than I am?"

Jay laughed. "You're like another category."

"So that's the week squared away." Mrs. D returned to her desk. "I've got your cell phone number, but I won't call unless there's an emergency."

Enrique said, "Go unplug. Rest."

Jay said, "I'm still seeing you tomorrow at the funeral."

Enrique hugged him. "Thank you. You know you don't have to come."

"I'm not dead yet," Jay said. "I'll be there even if I have to steal my brother's car to do it."

Kevin said, "Hey!" and Jay added, "Or take the bus. Something."

After Enrique left, Jay led Kevin down the creaky steps to his dismal apartment. In his bedroom doorway, Jay stopped and glared at the corner.

Kevin followed his gaze, then chuckled. "Oh, it's your new cat!"

"It's not my cat."

"It is now."

"I'm leaving, remember? Goodbye, cat."

Kevin picked up the bag on the bed. "Is this everything you're bringing?"

He hadn't meant to sound surprised, but the bag was light.

But really, what did Jay have? A weeks' worth of clothes, maybe? He wore the same thing all the time. Did he even have non-uniform clothing? Kevin hoped so. It would be awkward otherwise.

Jay lifted up a hard-sided case with a handle, and looking uneasy, he wouldn't let Kevin take that.

"Is that your little box of holiness?" Kevin quipped.

"Mass-in-a-Box." Jay sounded subdued. "Too bad it doesn't come with its own Priest-in-a-Box."

Kevin didn't like to think about Jay as the priest in a box, so he went upstairs, where it turned out Jay also had a backpack that weighed like he was transporting his coveted collection of cinderblocks. Jay hovered near Mrs. D's desk asking questions like a nervous parent until she shooed him out the door with, "It'll be fine. I've been in this job through three pastors already. I know what needs to be done."

And finally Jay was outside with Kevin in the rain, and Kevin brought his paltry luggage to the car. Jay kept the box on his lap, clutching the handle as though it were his vocation about to fly out the window.

They drove in silence, weaving through the city streets with the tires hissing against the runoff water, and then taking off once they reached the parkway. Shortly the graffiti-covered tenements yielded to cleaner row-houses and then cookie-cutter subdivisions.

So, was Jay still angry about the engagement ring thing? Or was he just gutted about leaving the parish for a few days? Did he really love it that much when it was destroying him?

Kevin said, "I went grocery shopping so you wouldn't have to hang out behind the local pizzeria."

Jay sounded flat. "I'm going to need you to write out your schedule. We don't have to be joined at the hip, but if I know when you'll be home, that would be better. And I'll need a bus schedule."

Kevin said, "I can drive you."

"Not to tomorrow's funeral. It's early."

"Where is it?"

"Devil's Corridor," Jay said.

"I'll call you a cab," Kevin said. "And an armed escort."

Jay rewarded him by smirking. "I live in the Devil's Corridor every day."

But that had broken the ice, so Kevin changed topics to the various amenities of his apartment. He had, for example, a television. Jay could use the WiFi, and there was the fitness center. "I hope you brought a swim suit."

Jay said, "Oh, yeah, about that. I hope you have an extra, otherwise we can't both swim at once."

Kevin chuckled. His brother was back. "How's Seth doing?"

"I waved my rosary and snapped my fingers and chanted in Latin, and now he's ready to sing lullabies in French to his teddy bears." Jay looked up as Kevin started laughing. "What's so funny?"

"You are. The kid's with you because you *are* trying to get through to him, and when I ask, that's what I get?"

Jay flipped the box handle back and forth. "You know how long it takes. And in my case, you knew what it took."

"He's got an advantage we didn't have."

Kevin hesitated because it sounded like he was accusing Jay of abandoning him, and that wasn't fair. He did have Jay back then, but he and Jay were only a year apart. What he'd meant was that the kid had an extended family, and neither Kevin nor Jay had that. But if he tried to correct himself, it would sound like he was trying to say they weren't family to one another, or that he was trying not to let Jay think Jay hadn't been enough for him back then, so instead of sounding like an idiot, Kevin chose to let the chips fall wherever they would.

Jay only said, "Whatever prayer and listening can achieve, that's what I'm doing for him. And maybe if I'm not there, he'll go home. It's hard to say. He said last night he'd follow me anywhere."

"First the cat," Kevin said, "then the kid."

Jay gave an aggravated eye-roll.

Kevin snickered. "I hope it doesn't crawl into a drawer and have kittens while you're away."

"You'll know," Jay said, "because when you get home from a night tour, they'll all be in your bed. Speaking of which, can I have an apartment key?"

Kevin laughed. They'd get through this week.

Although small, the apartment swallowed up Jay and his belongings. Kevin had wondered how Jay would store his things, but given the size of his duffle bag,

Kevin just combined the contents of two dresser drawers and gave Jay the empty one, and Jay stashed his Mass-in-a-Box in the bottom of the night stand. Kevin inflated the borrowed mattress and moved over his regular bed so there was space for the second one on the floor. Jay's toothbrush moved into the bathroom side by side with Kevin's. Kevin showed him the groceries, wrote down the WiFi password, and then got out their lunch—sandwiches. He'd even bought the good rolls.

"Before I go to work," he said, "let me show you where everything else is."

Begin the grand tour: the washing machines were in the basement, along with a refrigerated vending machine proudly proclaiming "_OLD FOOD" that theoretically dispensed chocolate bars and soda cans if propitiated with the correct currency. Outdoors, the complex was formed by a semi-circle of identical brown and white buildings dotted with covered porches. Kevin pointed out the rental office, the recreation center (proudly featuring both a pool table and ping-pong,) and the fitness center just outside the complex, with its indoor pool. "I'll leave the pass on the table."

"Sounds good," Jay said with the vigorous enthusiasm you normally reserve for a coupon that gave twenty-five cents off a three-pack of dental floss.

"I won't be home for dinner," Kevin said when they were back inside, "so make whatever you want, and you take the bed when you're ready to sleep."

"Are you sure?"

"The inflatable mattress is fine. I'm tough."

"You say that now," Jay quipped. "Tell me again in the morning. Speaking of which," he added, "will I be able to get out of there without waking you up?"

"It'll work," Kevin said. "I've lost sleep for less. I'm just glad to be able to help."

Twelve

Kevin would never, never, under any circumstances mind being awakened early so Jay could go to a funeral. *Of course.* So that first night, Jay left a change of clothes in the living room and kept his phone alarm on vibrate beneath his pillow. He shouldn't have worried, though. Unaware that he was on vacation, his circadian clock awoke him at dawn, and he crept out of the room without Kevin so much as changing his breathing.

Enrique had texted overnight that someone would pick him up for the funeral. Because it wasn't enough that the man had to plan his mother's burial: apparently he also had to play taxi dispatcher. Kevin had left a note on the kitchen table: he'd gotten in around two o'clock in the morning, so, "Have a nice day."

Jay turned on the coffee maker, then watched the sun peek between the two apartment buildings across the lot. For the moment, he had nothing to do. It felt wrong. He should find a book, start outlining a homily, and check his schedule to see who he needed to call first.

Instead it was just him and a coffee machine breathing out hot water with low-toned sighs.

What do you want from me? he prayed. *What can I do for Seth? For Enrique? What can I do for any of them from here?*

And how was he supposed to do what the bishop said and shave down his responsibilities to a miserable forty hours a week? The priesthood wasn't a job where you could just turn it off at the end of the day. It was more like what he heard single moms complaining about: the constant awareness of other people's dependency, all the time, every minute. You sit down to rest and you feel guilty because someone might be getting into something, or you have a muffin but your kid wants it, so you give it to him and then you have toast. And always, that mental division: you couldn't be just yourself because you had to be aware of wants the other person wasn't even aware of. *Thinking for two,* one woman had called it. Jay's job required thinking for seven hundred.

Still, the bishop had instructed him to figure out his priorities, so Jay tried.

Back in the army, his sergeant had raged about his commanding officers, "They keep bumping their own top priorities! Everything can't be top priority, can it?" That kind of made sense when lives were on the line. It made even more sense with souls. You didn't want someone to spend eternity in Hell because you brushed him off at one crucial moment.

So many people said they'd left the Church because of one individual. One hypocrite. One heartless comment. One mistake, and they took themselves out of the picture. Jay didn't ever want to be that one. He'd sooner die than be the reason someone left.

The coffee finished brewing, and Jay poured a cup. Kevin had bought the good stuff. Maybe he always bought the good stuff; maybe he'd gotten it just for Jay. Regardless, Jay resolved to fully enjoy it as a favor to his brother. *I think that's how we're supposed to give thanks,* Jay quipped to God, *by appreciating what we're given. So I'll appreciate this coffee.*

Jay texted his ride and asked when to be ready, then took out his not-yet-well-worn breviary and prayed morning prayer and the office of readings. He had a reply by the time he was finished, and long before Kevin would awaken, he'd gone outside to await the driver.

Jay's plan: funeral and graveside service, maybe attend the funeral lunch, and then take the bus to Saint Gus to check on things before finding his way back to Kevin's.

Jay's reality: he found himself surrounded by former co-workers and parishioners who were delighted to see him. They all, to a person, thought he'd lost too much weight and needed some rest. Both before and after the funeral (not during, thank goodness) Jay found himself engulfed by a stream of people who wanted to catch up. "Oh, Saint Augustine's! That's a tiny parish, isn't it?" "I've heard about your soup kitchen, but people always call it the Caf. What are you, a gourmet chef?"

With the faces and voices came memories: this parishioner's father was in a nursing home; that parishioner had a disabled child; these two had been cut off from their families due to their interracial marriage.

Each caught him up on his or her news, a few sentences followed by how good it was to see him again.

Jay had only been at OLQA for a year, so it was shocking that they knew him at all. But here they were, remembering.

"Don't be surprised," said the pastor on the drive back from the graveside. "Parishes become intensely loyal to their priest. I think that's why the diocese moves us around so much."

Jay said, "I don't like the *cult of personality* thing. Sometimes they do something because of us when they should do it because of Christ."

The pastor replied, "I suspect Christ accepts it anyhow, as if they'd done it for him."

At the funeral lunch, Jay took a seat at one of the empty tables, and quickly it filled. "Yo, I hear you're running a gang," said a guy named Mike. "Send them to me for a gun safety course. I'll teach them not to shoot themselves."

Jay shuddered. "I'm concerned enough about the knives. I don't want them getting guns too."

"They have them already," someone else replied. "They aren't telling you, but I guarantee they've got guns stashed in the rectory right now."

Jay wondered if Kevin could do a search with a K-9 officer. "House rules are to keep the violence off church property. They've been good about it."

"No target practice in the parking lot," the parishioner quipped, and Mike exclaimed, "Hey, that was a long time ago! We haven't done that in at least five years!"

Jay laughed.

Despite himself, he didn't dine-and-dash. He found himself relaxing.

"Are you sure you're safe at St. Augustine's?" said a woman named Clara. "I hear there are so many break-ins."

OLQA wasn't in a banner neighborhood either. Jay said, "We've had one break-in I really wish we could stop, but he keeps getting in. It's a black cat."

Everyone laughed around the table. "A cat burgler!" exclaimed Mike, and Clara added, "You've been chosen. That's what cats do."

Jay sighed. "I don't want a cat."

Carla put a hand on his arm. "I'm sure there are angels in charge of cats, and when they see a place one could live, they send a stray there."

Jay leaned closer to her and said, "How can we convince this angel to quit meddling?" and there was more laughter.

Enrique came and rested his forearms on Jay's shoulders, leaning over him. "You guys, this isn't an Irish funeral. You're not supposed to be laughing like drunkards."

"It's more honest this way!" Mike said. "Priests always look so dour. But look, we got him smiling!"

"Mom would be proud of that." Enrique pulled over a chair and sat next to Jay. "I'm sorry Mom didn't get a chance to meet you."

"We wouldn't have been mutually intelligible," Jay said with a smile.

"She spoke Cuban. You speak...well, good enough for a Spanish Mass." Enrique chuckled. "Between that and a few English words and maybe some sign language, you'd have gotten on great. If worse came to worst, she'd have taught you to make tortillas."

Jay said, "Fresh tortillas at the Caf."

Enrique said, "Maybe your brother watches the cooking network, but Mom's were better."

Carla said, "Oh, is your brother a priest too?"

Mike said, "Your brother and you didn't get on, did you?"

"We patched things up. I'm actually staying with him this week." Jay tensed as he told them about the enforced vacation, but no one said, "How dare you?" Instead, Clara and Mike and the others at the table said they were glad he would rest. "You look so tired," Clara said.

Mike added, "Seriously, get yourself a break. I know how hard you guys work."

Maybe the bishop (and Mrs. D, and Kevin, and Dr. Lacks) had seen something he couldn't. "I'm jumpy," Jay said. "I keep wanting to take care of something."

"There's no something to take care of here," Mike said. "Just a sandwich and chips you've got to eat."

"And tortillas," Enrique said. "You've got to learn to make your own. They're so much better than the stuff in bags."

When the church ladies began cleanup, Enrique brought Jay back to a table. "I got you a ride. My cousin is on the way back near where you're staying."

Jay said, "This is all so strange. I should be doing something."

"You're doing more than you know." Enrique hugged him. "Thank you so much for everything."

Everything.

Enrique's cousin entertained Jay by telling him how to make Grandma's tortillas, and after arriving at the apartment complex, Jay stood momentarily on Kevin's front steps, letting the sunlight warm him.

It was two o'clock. Kevin might have left already for work, but maybe not yet. Jay kind of wished he had. He loved Kevin, but sometimes he just didn't want to be with him. Or with anyone. The thousand people at the funeral had been awesome, but now Jay longed for quiet.

He let himself into Kevin's apartment only to hear the television in the living room and the shower pattering behind the bathroom door. In the kitchen, Jay poured a glass of water and looked out at the kids playing on the playground.

Tortillas and handguns. Black cats. Jay checked his phone, but Mrs. D hadn't texted him about any crises.

You're doing more than you know, Enrique had said, as though letting people take care of him was a huge effort.

Jay went into the bedroom to get his rosary, and on the bed was a Walmart bag with a pair of swim shorts that still had their tags.

Jay closed his eyes and shivered. Yes, letting people take care of him was a huge effort.

Thirteen

*H*aving Jay in the apartment was kind of like not having Jay in the apartment.

From their growing up together, Kevin thought of Jay as being all over the place all the time. If Kevin remembered watching TV, he remembered Jay sprawled on the other end of the couch. If Kevin remembered sticking dinner in the microwave, he remembered Jay at the table eating his own dinner of Peanut Butter Crunch. It was only now that Kevin remembered they did spend time apart. It always felt like they were always together, but how often had Jay been across the room playing a video game rather than watching TV with him?

They didn't feel together now. Kevin awoke at ten in the morning on Wednesday, and other than being on an air mattress alongside his real bed, he might as well have been alone. Jay had a talent for slipping out of the way. They'd seen each other for ten minutes yesterday between Jay's return from the funeral and Kevin's leaving for work. By the time Kevin returned, Jay had long since gone to bed (although Jay had left a note and a dinner to reheat if he wanted to).

This morning, Kevin couldn't hear Jay at all, but knowing he was there was all it took to ratchet up his senses, like climbing a dark stairwell, gun in hand, knowing the perp was in the building but not sure if he was armed.

When Kevin finally went into the kitchen, he found Jay at the table with his glasses on and books spread around him. While jotting notes in unsteady block print on a legal-sized yellow pad, he had a scowling concentration, probably because he had to focus hard to read the small type. He was wearing a regular t-shirt and shorts rather than the standard issue dog collar.

Jay had brewed a pot of coffee, so Kevin got himself a mug. "What are you doing?"

Grim-faced, Jay huffed. "I've got to prepare this weekend's homily."

Kevin chuckled. "It's kind of like divine revenge for all those times you didn't study. Now you've got to present a book report every Sunday."

Jay laughed, but it had a hollow sound.

Kevin leaned over him. "You're referencing everything. This isn't a scientific paper. What kind of citations do you need for 'Don't be a jerk'?"

"I can't pull a homily out of my head. I mean, I pray about it, but I also look up what everyone else has said. Usually something jumps out at me." The way Jay emphasized *usually* indicated it wasn't happening now. "Today I'm the first person in two thousand years not to have any thoughts whatsoever."

"Holly says every so often you get up there and say there isn't anyone in the church less qualified to tell other people how to live."

"I'm not wrong." Jay yawned, then flexed his shoulders. "You could come sometime if you want to hear me make a fool of myself. I'm sure it's a treat, and you'd have ammo for years to come."

Kevin laughed. "You make good coffee, by the way."

"You buy the good stuff, so it's easy." Jay started stacking his books. "Well, you're awake now, and it's clear I'm not making any headway. Do you need me out of here so you can have the place to yourself?"

"I didn't want to mention it, but my garage band is holding a rehearsal," Kevin said, "and afterward the Queen of England arrives for high tea."

Jay cracked a smile, maybe his first real one of the day. "Well, before you plug in your Gibson, want to head over to the gym?"

Kevin raised an eyebrow. "Okay."

He bolted down the rest of his coffee and changed into gym clothes. Other than a couple of women on treadmills and one old man on a recumbent bike, the fitness center was empty this late in the morning. Kevin pointed out the highlights. "That's the weight area, and here are the mats."

As Kevin turned away, Jay said, "Sounds good. But first—"

Jay tackled Kevin. With his back turned, Kevin was unprepared, and he yelped as he went down. Jay grappled with him, taunting at first and then threatening and finally struggling as Kevin got the upper position. Jay twisted with the roll and got himself on top long enough to toss his glasses to the side, then exclaimed protests as Kevin overpowered him again.

The ladies on the treadmills must have been appalled, if they could hear over their earbuds, but Kevin only laughed, holding back because he could so easily have pounded Jay into sand. Jay was still wiry, though, and once he slipped Kevin's grip even though Kevin was in much better shape.

Finally Jay couldn't continue, and he lay on the mat with his ribs heaving. Sweat glistened on his face.

Kevin disengaged. "You lunatic! Even at your best I could kick your behind!"

"What?" Jay stared at Kevin, open-mouthed. "Never!"

Kevin arched his eyebrows. "You're delusional."

"I let you win." Jay made his way to where he'd tossed his glasses, then staggered back to a seated position. The ladies on the treadmill weren't paying attention, but the man on the bike was chuckling.

Kevin sighed. "Now, Wonder Boy the Wrestling Priest of Doom, can we finally go for that swim?"

"Love to," Jay gasped.

They did laps in separate lanes, and it surprised Kevin how quickly he outdistanced Jay. In the middle of the third lap, Jay slowed dangerously and finally started treading water while reaching for the ropes. Kevin shot through the water and guided him to the side.

"I wore you out," Kevin said, a little breathless.

"I'm doing too much." Jay smiled like a rogue. "The bishop would kill me for this. I'm supposed to be relaxing." When Kevin started to speak, Jay said, "This is relaxing, believe it or not."

Jay pulled himself hand over hand to the ladder, not moving his legs. Kevin hovered close while Jay hauled himself onto the lip of the pool. "I think I'm finished for now."

Kevin started climbing out, but Jay shook his head. "I'm going to sit. You keep swimming."

"Maybe you could try the hot tub?"

Jay glanced at it. "Yeah, that might be okay." He tensed. "Mom's ring!"

Jay stared at his hand flared out in his lap, ringless. Horrified, he said, "It must have fallen off in the water—" and started to get back in.

"Don't be an idiot!" Kevin pushed him back. "You can't go diving. I'll look."

Jay shook his head, but Kevin said, "Remember what you said about that ring as an omen? I'm not having you die looking for it. I'll go. Get in the hot tub."

Kevin went underwater, opening his eyes to scan the pool bottom. A ring—such a tiny thing, but probably as big in Jay's mind as the engagement ring was in his.

He came up for air and Jay called, "Catch! I found a pair of goggles in the lost and found box."

Kevin fit them on, then proceeded down the lane, eyes on the bottom for the glint of metal. At the wall, right as he was about to give up, he found it.

He went to the bottom (not deep here at all) and picked it up, but as he did, he thought of how pale Jay looked at the poolside, how he'd pulled himself out of the water as though it took everything just to move.

He'd been hurt. The more fiercely Kevin pushed the thought away, the harder it slapped him when it returned: Jay was *disabled*. Jay was his brother, and Jay was disabled. While the Jay in his head scaled fire escapes at midnight with a spray paint canister in each hand, the Jay in reality leaned on a cane at the end of a long day.

This job. This job was killing him.

Kevin's hand tightened around the ring that Jay thought represented that very job.

He went to the hot tub. Jay had his eyes closed as he leaned against the side. His color had returned, but now he looked even more exhausted.

Kevin hadn't intended to kill him. He'd thought the pool would help.

Jay opened his eyes. "Did you find it?"

Without thinking, Kevin said, "No."

Jay looked devastated. "I'll tell them at the front desk. Maybe someone will find it and turn it in."

"Yeah, maybe." Kevin put the ring in his swimsuit pocket, then sat on the edge of the tub. "I didn't realize you were feeling this bad."

"You say it like I'm on death's door." Jay closed his eyes again and sank lower in the whirlpool. "Makes it all the more embarrassing the way I thrashed you."

"It's less embarrassing because it didn't happen." Kevin slipped himself in, relaxing as the heat soaked into his shoulders. "All kidding aside, if this much activity wore you out, maybe you need a longer break."

Jay shook his head. "If I can't handle my parish, they're going to pull me out and stick me in a desk job."

Kevin squinted. "Priests can have desk jobs?"

"What do you think the bishop does?" Jay shuddered. "Don't ever wish that on me, by the way. I'd make a terrible bishop."

Kevin shrugged. "Is that like being a police captain? How different would it be?"

Jay said, "It's the difference between owning a car and pumping gas. God didn't give me back my life to alphabetize files."

Kevin said, "Okay, then, so why did God give you back your life?"

Jay smirked because Jay always heard the things Kevin wasn't saying, and Kevin knew it. "Whatever it is, only God knows it right now. There were so many dispensations I needed to become a priest. Like Catholic waivers. I was too blind, too disabled, too everything. So I guess the bishop thought God had something in mind for me too."

Kevin said, "And does God get mad if you cut that thing out when you cut your hours?"

"I know, right?" Jay slumped deeper in the water and reached for where the gold ring should have been on his finger, then tensed when it wasn't there. "Everyone wants me to prioritize, but everything is top priority to someone."

Kevin laughed out loud. "Then you really have changed."

Jay looked surprised.

"If Dad gave you an order like that, you'd have said yes and then gone and done whatever the heck you wanted." Kevin leaned forward and pointed. "I can't believe you of all people aren't thinking of a way out of this."

Jay looked guilty.

Oh, man. Because if Jay knew Kevin, then Kevin knew Jay too. Of course he'd thought of a way out. Of course.

Kevin said, "Wait, back off a minute. You said you could go blind if you didn't gear down a bit. I know God and I aren't on the best of terms, but we'd both rather have you work at eighty percent for thirty years than one hundred percent for three."

Jay didn't reply.

Hope sparked inside. "Talk to me. Are you really going to quit?"

Jay looked shocked. "No, the point is *not* to quit. Okay, so let me give you a primer on playing the Catholic game. It's got rules, and some rules you can get out of, and some rules you can't. So you have to go to Mass on Sundays, but if it's a blizzard or if you're taking care of a sick relative, you don't have to go. On the other hand, if someone vows to be married, he can't decide to take a day off from being married. Following me?"

Jay looked uneasy. Calling his job a game? Maybe he really was questioning whether he should stay a priest. "I took vows when I was ordained," Jay said, "and one of them was obedience to my bishop. The bishop told me very clearly to cut down my hours."

"So you're trying to interpret it sideways," Kevin said, "to find a way out."

"He knows me too well. He was very explicit. Either I obey the order or else I flagrantly break one of my three vows." Jay bit his lip. It occurred to Kevin that if the point of a hot tub was to relax, Jay was doing the opposite. "But the Catholic trump card in all situations is pleading conscience."

Kevin said, "You're the only one who would conscientiously object to resting."

"It's just that conscience always takes precedence over obedience." Jay closed his eyes and shook his head. "But that's where I keep coming up short. My parish needs me, but is that pride? I need to work all-out as long as I possibly can, but is that a mistake? I mean, if you're going to follow your conscience, it has to be a well-formed conscience, and I haven't been doing this all my life."

This must be the kind of stuff Jay had in all those books. "People form their consciences?"

Jay nodded. "Oh, yeah. *Your* whole job is dealing with people whose consciences tell them it's okay to break the law. I've had people in my office who feel free to disregard every human norm you can imagine, including abusing their children. *I just don't see anything wrong with it.*"

Kevin sighed. "I suspect we've met the same people."

Jay rolled his eyes. "So yeah, of course we form our consciences. We read, and we pray. We ask for guidance from people with more experience. You must have done that when you joined the police force. *How do I handle a car chase? How do I get the perp to admit what he did?*"

Kevin said, "Do priests have mentors?"

Jay said, "I do, yeah," but in a really subdued voice. He stood. "I want to go look through the pool again. Maybe if I look—"

"You'll drown," Kevin said. "I can go back later, but you really shouldn't push any harder than you have."

It had never before occurred to Kevin just how slippery the tile floor could be, or how strange it was that the fitness center had no lifeguard. Jay kept looking back at the pool, but he didn't say anything more. They toweled off, then pulled on their t-shirts and went to the front desk. Jay reported the missing ring, and the bored woman behind the desk wrote his phone number on a yellow sticky note.

About halfway across the parking lot, Jay said, "I did call my mentor. He hit the ceiling."

Kevin groped in his mind. "About the conscience thing?"

"He doesn't want me to disobey. He wants me to at least go back to the bishop and try to compromise."

Kevin said, "That wouldn't work so well in the police."

"Father Ron figures I could counter-offer with however I plan to manage the stress if I keep working at a drop-dead pace. His words, not mine." Jay was walking slowly. "I'd been thinking about working out every other day if it helps this week."

Kevin said, "And you're going to find the time to do that...in your sleep?"

Jay sighed. "I can't just abandon my parish, but if I disobey, Bishop Sato can and will pull me from St. Gus faster than I can call a parish council meeting. But then again, if I really can't handle the parish, he's going to do the same thing, so what's the difference?"

Kevin huffed. "Sounds like the police force. They'll tell you to do something one way and then punish you for doing exactly what they said. *Here, take time off,* and then it's, *you took time off, so clearly you can't stay here.*"

Jay's hands tightened on his towel. "Organizations are like that."

Kevin said, "Then why stay with it? You made a promise to them, but don't they owe anything to you?"

Jay shook his head. "This is a lifetime gig."

"It doesn't have to be."

"I'm not leaving. The whole point is I don't want to do less of my job." Jay huffed. "The previous pastor hadn't done anything at all in quite a while, and because of that, we have pretty much zero volunteerism. They had a parish council that annually rubber-stamped an incorrect budget, and that was it."

Kevin's eyes narrowed "By comparison, you're like Mary Poppins, and they don't appreciate you."

"Father Ron says you and I grew up thinking it was all or nothing."

Jay was angry. This was an opportunity. "It *is* all or nothing. If you don't commit fully, why do it at all? What happens to St. Gus if you put up your feet and watch ESPN?"

"Right!" Jay's eyes brightened. "But he thinks I can motivate them by being involved at all, and because they love me."

"Aww," Kevin drawled. "So sweet."

"And I can demonstrate my eternal love by turning up every third meeting rather than every meeting. Shave fifteen minutes off each counseling session. Get someone else to run the youth group and make the volunteers run the Caf." Jay shook his head. "So why'd I even become a priest in the first place?"

Kevin nearly snapped that he didn't understand it either, but he caught himself in time. Instead he forced himself to behave like an officer. Jay was limping. Jay was exhausted. And as an officer, he said, "You tell me."

Jay answered in a thready voice. "The sacraments. I'd still be a priest even if I washed up on a desert island with only two palm trees for a congregation. That's what Father Ron says."

Jay sounded more broken than Kevin had ever heard, and even the officer inside Kevin couldn't keep hold of the brother in him right now. "Do you believe that?"

Jay wasn't even listening to him at this point. "He told me, *Get it out of your head that you're going to die for your people. Automartyrdom has never been recognized by the church.*"

Jay stopped speaking as they reached the apartment building.

"Here's what I don't get," Kevin said as he let them into the lobby. "You're loyal to them even though they're putting you in an impossible situation. They give you all this work to do, not enough resources to do it, and then order you not to do it after all. You said it's a vow, right? To obey? They know you won't break one of those." Wasn't that the reason he didn't want to marry Holly? Because he couldn't guarantee he wouldn't break a vow not to leave her, not when a bullet could force him to do it at any time. "So maybe you should push back. Or maybe God doesn't actually need priests to do His dirty work for him."

Jay didn't step inside the doorway. Kevin turned, but Jay was looking at him, baffled and hurt.

Kevin averted his eyes.

"I came here for help," Jay said, wavering. "That wasn't an invitation for you to attack me."

"I'm not—" Well, other than the fact that he was. Kevin sighed. "They're hurting you."

"It's not them. They want me not to hurt myself."

"Come in." Kevin's anger melted in the face of Jay's stung expression. "I'll back down."

As they went up the steps to the apartment, Kevin said, "You told Holly all that stuff about not working your way into Heaven. Then what exactly is it you're doing?"

Jay replied, "I don't know anymore."

"Well, trust me, I don't know either." Kevin unlocked the inner apartment door. "You want the first shower?"

Jay shook his head. "You're the one who has to leave for work. My work will wait for me on the kitchen table as long as it has to."

After showering and changing, Kevin walked into the bedroom without knocking. Just inside the door, he stopped when he found Jay lying on the bed, sleeping on his back like a ragdoll tossed aside. He must have been sitting and laid down for a moment's rest. One leg was tucked up under the other like a number four, and on that same side his arm was bent at a right angle. He'd dropped his towel at the foot of the bed like he always had years ago, but he'd put his glasses on the night stand. Without the glasses, he looked younger, fiercer, more familiar.

Kevin made his way to the gun safe on the wall and slipped Mom's wedding ring into the safe beside the other one. Jay didn't move.

All those years ago, Kevin had walked into a hospital room and found Jay wrapped in bandages and motionless in a coma. They'd flown to Germany in a panic, hoping they'd be in time to say goodbye but unable to do anything about the speed of the plane. Kevin had rushed into the room hoping to find Jay alive, but Jay hadn't been really alive right then. The machines said he was, but the machines were also the ones keeping him that way.

Kevin had anticipated mangled wreckage, and it had been this position he'd imagined. Jay bleeding, arms splayed, one leg pinned beneath the other and maybe even broken, his neck craned backward and his lips parted. But instead he'd found a false cleanliness—sterile bandages and white sheets. Stainless steel. Disposable single-use devices. Jay had been broken, but fully contained by an antiseptic neatness.

And here was Jay again, no longer contained but still broken. Not bleeding. Not dying except by parts.

This was the fault of the church, the fault of the bishop. Maybe even God's fault. But Kevin had seen too many domestic disputes to believe he could get in between them and force Jay to press charges in his heart. Not until Jay was ready to. And when things came to a breaking point, Kevin couldn't be the one who'd broken them because Kevin needed to be the one Jay fled to.

Kevin lifted the damp towel and draped it over the doorknob before backing out of the room.

Fourteen

Tik-tik-tik-tik-tik-ssssk-k-k-k-k...

On Friday morning, Jay awakened to a regular sound he couldn't quickly identify. He snuggled closer under the blanket and let the hiss and skip pervade his thoughts, still half asleep, until he recognized the lawn's automatic sprinkler system. Like a forgotten foreign language, it was the sound of sprayed water, the endless circling and returning of the sprinkler heads. *Tik-tik-tik-tik-tik-sssssk-k-k-k-k...*

Above that rhythm he heard dozens of birds he couldn't recognize by their cries alone. They could be seagulls and sparrows, starlings and cardinals, mockingbirds and bluejays. He was a city kid, and you never heard birds in the city. Pigeons and sparrows, sure, you saw those, along with an occasional bird you recognized as, "That's not a pigeon or a sparrow." He'd never realized how noisy they could get once you left the treeless zone. Kevin had never mentioned it.

Stretching, he squinted toward the windows and realized his face didn't hurt. He hadn't been frowning in his sleep.

He luxuriated in warmth a little longer, then crept out of bed to say morning prayer in the living room. That done, he opened the curtain before the kitchen's eastern-facing windows. He cleared everything off the table and shifted it so he could say Mass while the sun rose.

He was nervous in case Kevin "caught" him at it. But that made it all the more exciting, like a secret tryst with Jesus. If people could hold Mass in Soviet prison camps, surely he could handle having his brother walk in on him. If anything, Kevin would be the one embarrassed.

Afterward, delightfully awake with a good tingling rather than a numb one, Jay set up the coffee maker and then logged in to Kevin's computer to check his email.

The week had flown. Although they'd had to drag him out of St. Gus clawing at the pavement, Jay found himself reluctant to return. It was too easy to get accustomed to the nonstop leisure. Or rather, the non-pressure, because he was still active. Prayers and spiritual reading took up his early mornings, and after that he went to the gym with Kevin (although Jay was getting the impression that Kevin didn't go every day). The gym still hadn't turned up Mom's ring even though he asked every day, and that left him sad.

He'd explored Kevin's pantry and even done a little cooking rather than indulge in continuous meals of *MicrowavaBowl: Instant Dinner in Its Own Container!*™ Yesterday, he'd even experimented with Enrique's cousin's rendition of their family's tortillas. Kevin had regarded him in horror: "Jay, you're positively domesticated."

But for the most part, Jay reveled in the silences and the times he could just sit between activities rather than thinking in a panic that he'd forgotten something soul-shatteringly important to someone else.

At eight o'clock, Jay got a text from Enrique Hoyos asking him to call, followed by, "We had an incident at youth group."

Before Jay could call back, a second message arrived, this one a photo of a treadmill with a black cat curled on the belt, eyes gleaming gold as it stared into the camera.

Chuckling, Jay called Enrique. "Did that cat follow you home after youth group?"

"Nope." Enrique laughed. "That cat is pretty much yours forever. He just likes to sleep on the treadmill."

Jay said, "Where'd you take the picture?"

"Your creepy apartment, the unfinished side. At youth group, one of the guys said he'd found a freebie treadmill, so we took a field trip over to Mill Avenue and dragged the thing home."

Jay laughed out loud. "You did what?"

"No kidding. The boys took turns lifting the monster and stopping traffic so they could get it across Weston Boulevard, and after about an hour, one of them started saying, *Man, this thing better work,* and I was like, *You didn't even try it?* But it does work," Enrique said. "And your cat thinks it's comfortable. What's the cat's name? Do they need to be feeding it? Because they're not."

"It's not my cat," Jay said, "so call it whatever you like, and if you want to feed it, do that at your place."

Enrique sounded amused. "I've seen how this goes. You've got a cat. You might as well name him."

"Should I name him Lucifer, so I can expel him?"

Enrique said, "If you do that, after you've owned him a few years, some night he's going to stay out in the rain and the neighbors will see this deranged Catholic priest in the street calling for Lucifer to come home. Better name him something Latin."

Kevin came out of the bedroom, and Jay said, "Oh, I'm sorry, I didn't mean to wake you up."

Kevin shook his head and went into the bathroom. Jay turned back to the phone. "You had me worried when you texted that something happened at youth group. I didn't realize it was just that you'd started a treadmill shipping service."

"Oh, that wasn't what I wanted to tell you." Enrique still sounded relaxed, though. "Apparently there's some kind of bullying over at the middle school. One of the sixth grade Archangels is getting harassed by two eighth graders, and Masa went toe-to-toe with them yesterday."

Jay said, "The sixth grader, is it Esai?"

"Yeah. He's okay, just a black eye. Masa's in trouble, though, because even though the fight happened outside on Weston Boulevard, they're saying he had the knife on school property."

Jay rubbed his temples. "Is he getting suspended?"

"The school wants to talk to you, and that may be what about. Mrs. D asked if I could do it, and I'm cool with that. But you know them better."

"I'll talk to them." Jay shook his head. "Did he hurt the other kids?"

"Apparently, but I don't know how bad. He says something bigger is going to go down at the school today, and he's strutting around like it's a badge of honor."

Of course he is. Jay sighed. "Well, thanks for telling me. I'm sorry you had to deal with it so soon after losing your mother."

"I'm just glad I could be there. You enjoying your time off?"

"I am." Jay sounded more mystified than he intended. "Don't worry, though. I won't get used to this. I've got to be back tomorrow night."

"Well, enjoy what's left. Let me know what happens with Masa."

Jay put down the phone as Kevin joined him in the kitchen. "I'm sorry I woke you up."

Kevin shook his head. "I made an arrest last night and need to be in court this morning, so I'm going in early."

"Oh, that's convenient. Can I catch a ride with you?"

Kevin shrugged. "Sure, but you're still coming back tonight, right? Holly planned a movie night. Pizza, chips. The whole thing."

"Sounds great." Jay nodded. "There's a meeting at the middle school, so you can drop me off near one of the bus lines."

A meeting. Not a meeting as much as the parochial equivalent of what Kevin was about to do in the courthouse. He'd get a hearing with Sister Magdalena, the thousand-year-old mother superior of the Oblates of Mary Immaculate who ran the school, a woman who struck equal measures of fear and devotion into the hearts of her students. You did not want to go head-to-head with Sister Magdalena, and yet Jay suspected he was about to do exactly that.

Still, he found himself looking forward to it. Had only a few days' rest done that much for him? Because instead of feeling furious with Masa and frustrated with Esai and aggravated at the school for permitting the bullying in the first place, instead he felt moderately amused. Optimistic, in fact. Masa was his parishioner. So was Esai. And he was going to advocate for them.

In the car with Kevin, the conversation never stopped. Jay told him about the treadmill and the cat (and Kevin started suggesting names). Kevin laughed out loud at the image of all these gang members hauling exercise equipment across some of the neighborhood's busiest streets, and Jay said, "Poor Enrique! I guarantee you, he's wishing he hadn't asked us for money after all."

"How's Seth doing?"

Jay said, "That kid. He's been texting me on and off. I'm surprised he didn't turn up on your doorstep, to be honest. His grandmother called him but she says his voice sounds like his father's, so she hung up."

"Charming people."

"I have Mrs. D phoning other relatives he can live with, at least on a temporary basis. His father's sister is the executor, so even though the will specifies the grandparents as his guardians, they might be able to get him out of there." Jay sighed. "Seth inherits everything in trust, but since it's in trust, his legal guardian gets control for now. The grandparents don't want to be reminded of their son, but I guess their son's money might be something of a balm to their wounded spirits."

"I need to go to seminary," Kevin said in a reverent hush. "That way I tell a judge *balm to their wounded spirits* the same way you do."

"I'll sign you up," Jay said. "They'll also teach you to say things like, *Get that cat out of my apartment.*"

Kevin shot back, "*Ramen noodles are great for two meals: the noodles for lunch and the broth for dinner!*"

Jay said, "*No, by all means, time my homilies with a stopwatch. It helps my self-esteem.*"

Kevin said, "What was that thing your mentor said, about self-immolation?"

Jay exclaimed, "Martyrdom, not immolation! *Automartyrdom isn't recognized by the Church.*"

"Automartyrdom. I'll remember it in case I'm ever on a game show. *What has never been recognized by the Catholic Church? Kevin?*" Kevin laughed out loud. "Then I win a million bucks. You're training me just fine!"

Jay snickered. "First lesson's free. Oh, and you'll also need to renounce all your worldly possessions and maybe believe in God. Let me know when that begins to look appealing."

Kevin pulled up at the bus stop in front of City Hall. "You'll be the first to know. Call me when you want me to pick you up."

"When do you get off shift?"

"I'm just here for court. After it's done, I'll be pretty much free to go."

Jay went to the bus shelter while Kevin drove off to find a parking spot, and when the bus came, the driver put his hand over the fare slot. "It's on me, Father."

Jay thanked him and found a seat in the third row just as his phone rang. His father's name appeared on the screen, and he answered, "Dad?"

"Jay! Don't sound so surprised. How are you doing?"

"Pretty good." The nearly empty bus crept through downtown, and Jay gazed out the window at the uncrowded streets. The commuters had arrived at their offices by now, and it made for a nice change. "What's going on?"

"I wanted to catch you and Kevin together. Has he left for work yet?"

"Actually, he has a court appearance this morning," Jay said, "and I'm on a bus going to do battle with a nun who's seen it all."

"Oh." Dad sounded disappointed. "I thought it would be fun to talk to you both at the same time."

"We'll both be back there this afternoon." Jay hesitated. "Is it something important?"

"I never get to hear you both together. You weren't talking to each other for so long, and I just liked the idea of my boys being in the same house." Dad sounded suddenly graver. "I wasn't around much when you were growing up, but I miss spending time together."

Jay stared out the window at a mother walking with her child's hand in hers.

"I wish we had those years back," Dad said. "I could have been a better father."

No one was near enough to hear Jay over the grumble of the bus engine, but Jay prickled with self-consciousness. "I think we turned out okay."

"You both did. I'm real proud of you."

Jay said, "If you're around, you can try catching us this afternoon."

"I will. You wearing your mother's ring?"

Jay looked at his finger where the ring should be, and he managed to say, "When it came, I put it right on."

"Good. She'd be proud of you too."

Jay's heart sank.

"Just don't mention the engagement ring to Kevin. He wasn't too pleased."

"I got that impression myself when he chewed me out." Dad laughed. "Call me when you're both in the same place."

"I will," Jay said as the middle school came into view. "I love you."

"I love you too. Talk to you later today."

I love you. Walking into the school, Jay turned the words over in his head. Of course that's what you said to your father. Jay whispered it at the altar, too, when he said Mass. *I love you.* Christ, who had loved him enough to create him and then put up with him—Christ deserved to hear it. Jay loved Kevin too, but he couldn't recall ever saying it. That wasn't the kind of thing they did. If Jay ever did say it, Kevin would probably think he was about to die.

I love you, Jay prayed. It felt right.

The middle school felt like a stronghold among the tenement housing. The church it was attached to had sprung up in a crowded immigrant community sixty years ago, and then the neighborhood had crammed itself around it, and eventually the church had disappeared. The school itself had become something of a magnet, and most of its too-few students were there on scholarships provided by rich suburban parishes.

Like the row houses on the rest of the block, the school was three stories tall and shoulder-to-shoulder with the adjacent buildings, its schoolyard completely enclosed by all the apartments. The building stood an entire ten feet back from the road, bordered by twelve-foot-high wrought iron fences topped with double-coiled razor wire.

At the front entrance of this educational fortress, the school's public safety officer greeted him with a handshake. "Who loves you, Father Jay?"

"You do, Ben," Jay said with a grin. "You keeping the kids in line?"

"They're good kids," he said, winking. "It's hooligans like you that I need to watch out for."

Ben didn't even know the half of it. "Will you let me in anyhow?"

Ben gestured for him to go on past. He was a former police officer who'd taken a security job after retirement. Who knew: maybe someday Kevin could do this, although probably not. Jay imagined it was long hours of boredom punctuated by moments of shallow human interaction.

When Jay walked into the office, the school secretary got a bemused grin, and Sister Magdalena frowned at him. "Go away. You keep bringing us trouble wearing red armbands."

"I tell them not to wear the things on school property." Jay walked past the sign-in desk. "And I absolutely do not condone them bringing weapons. Let's talk."

The nun wore a head covering but not a habit. Instead she wore a blazer over a button-down shirt and a wool skirt. Her black eyes glared right at Jay, who met her stare smiling easily. Sister Magdalena belonged to a generation of nuns that automatically deferred to a priest's opinion, but never had done so herself. The result was this spark of a woman who always acted in the best interests of her school, so when Jay pressed her to do a favor for his boys, whenever she conceded anything, he knew she believed it would be a good thing.

"I only got part of the story," Jay said, "and I got that from someone who only got part of the story from Masa while they were carrying furniture across town. So I'd like to hear from you what actually happened, and then we can work out the consequences."

"I can handle Masa." Sister Magdalena waved a hand dismissively. "When he's not showing off, he's respectful and smart and a hard worker. I wish we had a whole school full of Masas." Sister Magdalena strode to her office, and Jay followed. "This is the problem."

Jay found himself facing Seth.

"How'd you get here?" he exclaimed, but Seth was busy exclaiming the same thing.

"He isn't enrolled," Sister said, "and while I appreciate the touch of him wearing the school uniform, it's not clear to me how they thought they'd sneak him in."

Masa's experience in public school might have led him to believe the teachers didn't pay attention to who attended class. Masa might even have been right. Seth was wearing a uniform that was too big on top and too small on bottom, maybe cobbled together from different kids' spares. And on his arm, he sported a red armband.

"You can't come here," Jay said.

"This is the school everyone else goes to."

Most homeless kids didn't consider school attendance a priority. "It's not a public school. You have to be formally admitted, and then there's tuition."

Seth said, "It's a Catholic school. The Church welcomes everyone."

"Our little lawyer will fit in great," murmured Sister Magdalena. "I even know which teacher to inflict him on. But he can't just show up."

"Esai said you get visitor students," Seth said, "so that's what I am. I'm visiting."

"You're wearing a gang armband," Jay said.

"Masa wears his."

"Masa gets regular detentions for that, too." Sister Magdalena walked around to her side of the desk. "We can start the admission paperwork, but until you're admitted, Mr. Cantrel, you aren't a student here."

"I'm a *pilgrim*," he snapped.

"You're a *trespasser*," Jay replied mildly. "How are you doing, by the way?"

"Pretty good. Did that Hoyos guy tell you about the treadmill?"

"He sent me a picture. I didn't know treadmills came with a cat attachment." Jay sat in the seat alongside Seth's. "So let's back up a bit. Yesterday, Masa got in a knife fight after school. He cut a fellow student who had been bullying Esai and said worse was still to come. And today, you're desperate to start school." Jay rubbed his chin. "We must admit that it's an intriguing connection."

"Ah!" Sister Magdalena smiled. "Which one are you trying to protect?"

Seth swallowed hard.

Jay said, "Were you there when Masa started the fight?"

"Look, it wasn't like that," said Seth. "The other kid had a knife too. When the kid pulled his blade, Masa tackled him, and the kid ended up cutting himself. They threatened to kill Esai. They said they know his schedule and he'd better watch himself and all that. I promised I'd stay with him, but then the music teacher sent me down here."

"No one wants Esai to get hurt," Jay said. "But there are better ways to handle it."

"Like what? Tell the school? They haven't done jack squat for him so far."

Sister Magdalena's eyebrows raised. "Has he asked for help?" She turned to Jay. "Have you spoken to us about this issue?"

"I heard about it for the first time this morning, so I'm going to assume if the school hasn't done jack squat it's because you've been asked for exactly that much." Jay opened his hands. "We can't fix what we don't know about."

"We can handle this," Seth said.

"Masa nearly handled it by getting stabbed."

"He was fine," Seth grumbled.

Sister Magdalena said, "I'll speak to Esai. I've already gotten a call from the parents of the boy who got hurt last night, and they'll be here this afternoon. They're alleging that the Archangels are bullying their son, and we'll need to detangle the situation. In the meantime, I alerted all the teaching staff to prevent any interactions between the parties, and to closely monitor the interactions that are inevitable. Fortunately, those families seem to have kept their boys home today, and every Archangel except these two are playing hooky, so that won't be a problem."

Jay frowned, envisioning a gang brawl away from the school. "Is Masa here?"

"Masa is in...art."

Jay turned to Seth. "I appreciate that you want to help them. I really do, and you're generous."

"Don't give me that!" Seth's eyes flared, and Jay thought there might even have been tears. "I can't let them get hurt! They're my family now!"

Jay reached for him, but Seth jumped from the chair, knocking it backward. "You've got to let me stay with Esai!"

Sister Magdalena started saying, "We can—" but didn't get to finish. From the hallway came a bang and shattering glass.

Jay dove for Seth with the long-forgotten instincts from Iraq, the sound triggering memories and fears and at the same time the certainty that he'd just heard a bomb. He shielded Seth with his body, while two more explosions came one after the next.

"What was that?" Seth exclaimed.

Jay pushed him toward Sister Magdalena. "Get him under the desk and keep him there. I'll come back if it's safe."

Seth lunged after him, but a fourth explosion sounded. Sister Magdalena with an iron hand shoved him under the desk.

Jay opened the door into the front office to find it filled with smoke. "Get into her office," he yelled to the secretary. "Call the police. Stuff something under the door."

"I called a lockdown," the secretary said. "Don't go out there!"

"Get in there!" Jay opened the door into the hallway.

Smoke roiled around him. The intercom blared out a brain-numbing alarm to shelter in place, but it made him want to run rather than hide. The smoke was greyish-white, not black. A student barreled into him, her ponytail flying behind her, tears streaking her face. "Here!" He pulled her to the office door. "Into Sister Magdalena's office. Stay with her."

Jay took off through the smoke toward the classrooms.

Kevin and Bill were laughing with some friends from the 35th precinct on the court house steps. "So I pull him over," Bill was saying, "and mention the busted taillight. The perp tells me, *It's not my car!* Then I run his license, and it turns out there's an arrest warrant. *It's not my ID!* We search him, and there's a gun in his jacket. *It's not my gun!* We cuff him and search the car, and there's drugs. *Not my drugs!*"

The radio blared, and the dispatcher said, "10-17, copy, 299 West 22nd Road, active shooter at Municipal Catholic Middle School, copy. Caller is indicating someone is shooting in the building and multiple detonations. All units respond to the school."

"Jay!" Kevin turned. "My brother's there! Where's the car?"

The guys from the 35 said, "Get in ours."

Bill said, "I'll grab the sergeant and follow. Go!"

Kevin jumped into the back seat and was dialing Jay even before the squad car had fully accelerated. The phone rang twice, and when Jay answered, Kevin could hear alarms.

"Jay, so help me, get out of there."

"Masa and Esai are upstairs."

"Let the good guys take care of it," Kevin urged. "We're on our way. We're breaking the sound barrier."

Between the siren on the squad car and the alarm in the school, it was a wonder Jay could hear him at all. Jay said, "We don't have the time. I heard gunshots."

Kevin said, "You're not armed! You can't do anything!"

Jay said nothing. Kevin shouted into the phone, "Don't be an idiot! Automartyrdom has never been recognized by the Church!"

Jay said, "I love you." And then he hung up.

Kevin closed his eyes. Beneath the patrol car, the four tires consumed the pavement and it was still far too slow. Every couple of minutes, the dispatcher gave more information in terse tones. More gunfire. School in lockdown.

"Automartyrdom?" said the officer in the passenger seat. "Where'd you learn to talk like that?"

"Seminary." Kevin swallowed hard. "It rubs off on you."

The two guys from the 35 scorched up the boulevard, and Kevin inched forward as though he could arrive faster. By the time they pulled up at the school, eight patrol cars were all over the street. Kevin bolted for the incident commander.

He showed his badge. "Kevin Farrell, 42nd precinct. My brother Jay is inside the building. I want you to send me in."

"We can't get close." The captain pointed to the third floor. "Snipers in the corner windows. We're sending a team through the houses on the other side to break in through the school yard and the roof, but right now they're locked down tight."

Kevin dialed Jay again. Jay needed to get out of the line of fire. Kevin had nearly lost him once all those years ago. It couldn't happen again, not now, not so suddenly, not when they were this close to everything being okay.

"He's an Iraq veteran," Kevin said, but his voice sounded as though it came from someone else.

The phone kept ringing, and Jay didn't pick up.

Fifteen

The alarms cut out, and Jay's ears rang with the silence.

Kevin had called again, and Jay refused to pick it up because Kevin would order him out of there, but Jay nearly answered just to tell him to stay away. You don't send your little brother in this kind of situation. There might be dead kids. There might be anything.

The loudspeakers flared into life, Sister Magdalena with her I Am a Nun voice that could bring an entire school to attention: "We are in lockdown. This is not a drill. The police and fire department are en route. All lockdown procedures are in effect."

Seth was with her. At least he'd be safe.

Jay rounded the corner and came on a body.

Oh, God, please, no...

It was Ben. Ben, the crinkle-eyed security officer. He had a gunshot wound to the chest.

Jay tried with shaking hands to get a pulse, but he couldn't find any. So he made the sign of the cross on Ben's forehead and whispered, "By the authority granted me by the Holy See, I impart to you a plenary indulgence and the remission of all your sins; and I bless you in the name of the Father, and of the Son, and of the Holy Spirit."

He didn't even know if Ben was Catholic. Let God figure it out.

Ben's radio beeped. "Officer Lestone, please respond."

Jay removed the radio from its slot and hit the button. "This is Father Jay Farrell. Officer Lestone is down, gunshot to the chest, likely dead."

Long hesitation, and then, "Farrell, give your location."

He was back in the army. "I'm in the first floor stairwell on the far side of the school from the main entrance." Ben had been in the main entrance. He must have run toward something—either toward the classrooms or else chasing someone. His gun remained in its holster.

Jay could take that and defend himself. But...killing someone? Even to save a kid, how could he?

"Father Farrell," said a different voice, "this is Captain Montrose, incident command. Please take shelter."

"Negative. I have students upstairs, and you don't have anyone else in the building."

"Sir, you're in danger, and your brother is standing right here. You need—"

"It would take a very special kind of fanatic to shoot a priest," Jay said. "This has to be inter-gang violence, and they don't want me. They want the Archangels."

"Oh! You're *that* priest."

Jay said, "Why aren't you in here yet? There are two hundred students in lockdown and at least one dead."

"They've got snipers in the corner classrooms to fire on all approaches. We're calling in a SWAT team."

"ETA?"

"Five minutes."

Jay chilled. So many kids could die in five minutes. "The corner over the main entrance is a library. The far corner will be the art room."

"The radio you have, that's private issue. If you're not going to leave," said the captain, "then hit the blue button on the front. That turns it into a receiver. Dial up the sensitivity. If I can hear your heartbeat, that's just about right. Narrate as you go. Tell me who is where, how many, everything tactically important. Your brother tells me you're a veteran."

Fiddling with the radio, Jay said, "Did my brother tell you I'm stubborn too?"

"That's the nicest thing he said. Don't engage, but if you insist on going upstairs, I want all the information I can get."

Jay pushed the button and shoved the unit in his pocket. "I'm heading in. No more gunfire and no one's moving."

The stairwell air was marginally more breathable. Whatever the attackers had done, it left a heavy smoke that wanted to go to ground. The building had only one stairwell, and Jay moved upward, keeping as quiet as possible.

On the second floor, the teachers and the students had all done a disappearing trick while the entire floor maintained an otherworldly silence. At this time of day, the tiled hallway should have reverberated with good-natured talk and the sounds of adolescent bodies writing or fidgeting in boredom.

"No activity on the second floor," he said. "Proceeding to third."

Third floor had the music and chemistry classrooms, the library, and the art room. Masa had been in art. Seth said Esai was in music. And the first bombs had been set off by Archangel-hunters.

Steps beneath. Jay froze. "You down there," he called. "Lockdown! Now!"

Had some kid got trapped outside his classroom? Would the teachers just hide inside, doors locked, letting a student die in the hallway because of an ill-timed bathroom break? Should he go get that one?

Above, someone shouted, "Don't move or you're dead!"

That made his decision for him. The one downstairs would hear it too and stay put. Jay called, "I'm Father Jay Farrell of Saint Augustine parish, and I'm here for my parishioners."

"I don't care who you are! Come closer and I'll shoot!"

Given the age of the voice, Jay figured the kid was more likely to hit him if he fired a warning shot than if he aimed for the heart. Jay said, "You gonna kill a priest? I'm not armed."

"Stay there!"

The kid's voice wobbled just enough to make up Jay's mind. He climbed through the remaining smoke. "Go ahead and shoot. It won't be anything that hasn't happened to me before." Jay advanced, keeping one hand on the banister. "Are all of you up here on the third floor?"

"I told you to stay down!" The kid sounded frantic. "Mike! Eric!"

One boy would freeze, but more boys might conceivably provoke one or the other to fire, so Jay closed the rest of the distance. "I told you, I'm not armed. I'm a priest. Priests give last rites. You killed that guard downstairs, you know."

Outside, Kevin would be beside himself. Kevin would be urging into the radio, "Don't go up there! Are you stupid?" to which Jay would have to respond, "I'm pretty sure I've cornered the market on that."

Kevin, always angry at him. But angry because of fear. *Don't you get it?* he thought as if to Kevin. *I'm petrified too.*

A second kid appeared beside the first on the landing.

The first looked at the second, horrified. "Eric killed the security guard!"

"Ben Lestone. Now you know his name." Jay reached the top. "Search me for weapons if you want. I don't even have my sick call kit."

He spread his arms, and after exchanging glances, the boys decided Mike should pat him down. No gun turned up. Jay said, "You need to bring me to anyone who's hurt or dying. I don't care what argument you have with the cops. My job is administering the sacraments."

Mike said, "Bring him."

The younger one said, "But—"

Mike exclaimed, "He's another hostage, moron! Don't bring him to Eric. Eric will kill him. And you too, for letting him up. But the cops won't bomb the building if there's a priest inside!"

Jay imagined incident command making all sorts of remarks at his expense. "Just bring me to anyone who's injured or dying."

Mike pointed his gun at Jay. "You walk ahead of me. Go to the library."

"There's blood in the hall." Steady. Get the information back to the police. "Is anyone hurt in the music room? Let me in there."

"There isn't," said the younger one. "We made them go to art."

Hear that? Jay thought to Kevin. *You've got a room with just one sniper holding it. You could tear-gas that in a heartbeat.*

Jay said, "What's your name?"

The younger one said, "Tim."

As he walked, Jay said, "Anyone hurt in 302?" *No,* answered Tim. *Keep moving,* said Mike. "And no one is hurt in 303? How about 304?" *Keep moving.*

The police needed to know where everything was. Jay said, "So it's just the art room and the music room? Just the two of you are holding the whole school?"

"There's more of us!" Mike must have been a seventh or eighth grader. He didn't carry himself like a teen, but he wasn't a child. "There's lots more! Keep moving!"

Jay glanced at the locked doors. "You're hunting for Archangels members. You know which classes they're in right now because they're your classmates. So you set off smoke bombs to force a lockdown."

They'd reached the art room. Jay swallowed hard. "And then you broke into only those rooms because you knew which rooms would have the Archangels in them."

Mike said, "You think you're smart. Want a medal?"

"I want my sick call kit. I can't anoint without oil." Jay braced himself, and he opened the door.

The smell of gunfire and blood's nauseating scent hit him like a wall. For a moment he was in Iraq, back in a pulverized jeep with one of his buddies tossed over him and the numb realization that this was death, and that he was leaving this world.

"Father Farrell!" He came back to the present at the mix of student voices and at least one teacher voice. "Get out of here!"

Jay rushed to the nearest form and crouched down, hands on his body. An adult. The art teacher?

A kid was aiming a rifle out the window. He shouted, "Why'd you bring him in here?"

Mike made himself sound tougher. "He's a priest. He'll make a good hostage."

"Hostage how?" The kid with the rifle didn't turn from the window. "Who's going to kill a priest?"

The teacher seemed to have a wound to the abdomen, blood all over him, all over the floor. Jay made the sign of the cross over the man's head, once again murmuring the apostolic blessing. Again, he had no idea if this man were Catholic. Let God check the paperwork.

He should report something to the cops. Some kind of intel. It was so hard to think. He said, "There are twenty-five students in here." So much more he should say. The students were in the corner, frightened into silence. There might be another teacher among them, maybe not injured. He couldn't tell.

The teacher reached for his hand. Jay squeezed. It was slippery, but he gripped tight and felt a ring, maybe a wedding ring. "I'm going to help your students. Stay down. I'll take it from here."

That's what the police said to one another. They seemed to think it helped.

It was a nightmare. He moved to the next unmoving form, and it was Masa. "Masa," he whispered into the radio. Blood on his face. Blood on his upper arm and soaking through his uniform shirt.

Masa was curled around himself, hand pressed to the wound, eyes closed. "I need water and towels. Isn't this an art room?" He reached for the stack of microfiber squares himself and pressed one up against Masa's arm. Then he traced the sign of the cross on Masa's forehead while saying the apostolic blessing.

Below him Masa's eyes opened, and he winked.

Okay, he was alive. The stupid kid had done that trick he'd talked about, where you make it look like you have a head injury. The stab wound on his arm—that was real, but it wasn't fatal. He'd gone down and made himself look dead because you don't shoot a dead body.

The gunman at the window (gunman? Was he even thirteen?) kept his eyes outside. "Watch that priest. I've heard things about him."

The next child, presumably dragged here from the music room, was Esai. And this wasn't fakery: Esai had been shot in the shoulder.

"Hey, open your eyes." Jay grabbed a water bottle off a desk. "Esai, stay with me!"

His heart raced, and his grip slipped because his hands were already covered with the blood of three people. Not Esai. Not like this.

Esai seemed serene, slipping behind a psychic barrier of blood loss. *He's here because of me,* Jay thought in a panic. *If I hadn't gotten him into this school—if I hadn't allowed the Archangels to adopt St. Gus in the first place—God, save him, save him, please.*

"You're good, man," Esai murmured. "I got you that treadmill. You owe me."

"Hang on. That's not a fatal wound. We'll get help. Esai, look at me." He locked Esai's gaze in a stare. "Esai, it's time to stop bleeding."

Esai didn't look away. "Okay."

Jay clutched his water bottle. "You want to be baptized?"

Closing his eyes, Esai nodded.

So Jay did it right there. He poured the water, said the words, made the sign of the cross and inadvertently left a blood-stained plus sign on Esai's forehead. Life among death while a bunch of teens pretended to be soldiers and the real soldiers couldn't do a thing.

He'd give anything right now if Esai could live. His work, his parish, his desires—they didn't matter in comparison to this. To Esai and to all these kids who needed to live. To live here, and to live eternally.

One of the students called across the room, "Is he gonna die?"

"Shut up!" shouted Mike. "Whoever talks is next to get it!"

Jay applied direct pressure to the shoulder wound, hoping it would clot. Why wasn't it stopping? Why couldn't he remember field triage, entry and exit wounds, all that? Why did it smell like a battlefield? Why was there gun smoke in a classroom?

He raised his head and looked to the kid with the rifle. "If you're keeping hostages, why the hell aren't you negotiating? You're not supposed to let everyone die. Don't you know how this kind of thing even works?"

The kid with the rifle said, "Shut up before I shoot you in the mouth!"

Jay's voice verged on hysterical. "Didn't you have a plan for getting out of here?"

And he realized then, they didn't. They'd had a plan, kind of. Get into position. Set off smoke bombs on the bottom floor while the ones upstairs laid in wait outside two specific classrooms. When the students came out of the rooms, they'd kill the ones they wanted to kill. And then what...? They could mix in with the panicked students, lose themselves in the shuffle, and then melt away into the city.

But something went wrong with their plan because it hadn't been a very good plan to start with. The main office had ordered a lockdown, not a fire alarm. So the attackers found themselves in a standoff, and they had no idea how to get out of it.

And for what? For a red armband?

Jay said, "You guys, if you call the police, you can talk to them. You can get out of this before it goes any further."

Tim, the youngest, said, "Really?"

The one with the rifle said, "And what are they going to do? Land a helicopter on the roof and give us a flight to Mexico?"

Jay said, "Why don't you ask?"

"Oh, yeah, the cops will totally talk to me."

"They'll talk to me!" Jay leaned up taller, but he didn't want to take his hands off Esai. "Put me on the phone, and I'll negotiate for you."

Tim whispered, "Eric would never."

Jay said, "Get Eric in here. Let's get this settled. The only way these shootings end is in suicide, and I don't want you dead either. If you don't want to save Esai's life, save your own. Get Eric in here. Get me on the phone with the cops."

Tim stayed frozen. Mike slapped him in the shoulder and said, "Go! Get Eric!"

Tim fled.

Jay fought to steady his breathing. The microfiber towels had soaked through, and he grabbed another handful. Hands turned red in blood and white uniform shirts turned red, but these little towelettes turned black. They should have been for spreading wood stain or smudging conte crayons, and instead this. This. *Esai. God, have mercy on Esai.*

"What are you doing?" This was the fourth voice, the lunatic Eric, the one they seemed to think would kill everyone just because, and probably the one who shot Esai. The one who killed Ben. Jay's teeth clenched.

"Where's Tim?"

"I put him in the stairwell. I heard someone." Eric pointed his gun at Jay. "Who's this? Our professional negotiator?"

Mike said, "He's going to get us a helicopter."

Before Jay could object, Eric said, "And you believe him?"

Jay said, "Do you have a plan to get out of here alive? Because if you do, I suggest you start it."

"Is that loser still alive?" Eric handed Mike his rifle and took the handgun. "I thought he was good and dead."

Jay said, "And once you've finished shooting Archangels, is your plan to shoot your comrades and yourself so it's all neat and tidy?"

Mike said, "That's not true! We're going to get out and go somewhere else!"

Jay said, "He has no exit plan except having a pretty standoff and shooting you all right before the cops charge in."

The kid at the window aimed his rifle right at Jay. "Why don't you shut up?"

Jay said, "Sure, point all your guns at me! Three people to take down a disabled priest? Why not? You thought revenge would be cool. But it stopped being a game when you killed Lestone."

Mike backed away from Eric. "Don't shoot the priest! He's going to get us out of this."

Jay kept direct pressure on Esai's chest. Stop bleeding. Stop. "Don't aim that gun away from me, Eric. Your friend admitted you don't know what I'm capable of."

Please let the cops be listening. *Please. Kevin, now. Come in now.*

Eric stepped forward. "You want to die? Because that's the way you die."

Behind him, the window exploded.

Jay flattened over Esai, horrified that a police sharpshooter had taken out a thirteen year old from the ground level. They'd held off for so long. Why not longer?

"Drop that thing!"

The voice came from behind him, and it wasn't a SWAT team. It was Seth.

What was he doing here? Had those been his steps in the stairwell?

Seth barreled past Mike, smacking Mike with the side of his handgun and then tackling Eric.

The kid at the window fired, but the bullet went wild. A ceiling fluorescent exploded in a blizzard of glass, and Seth slammed Eric in the side of the head with the handgun.

That gun in his hands: that had to be Ben's.

Seth head-locked Eric and put the gun against his temple. "I will not miss," he shouted. "Drop your weapons!"

Jay shouted, "Seth, no!"

Seth had gotten past the kid in the hallway and come in here to be a hero. Save the people he couldn't save before.

Seth kept the kid head-locked. "I said put the weapons down!"

Mike dropped Eric's rifle. The kid at the window got to his feet with his rifle trained on Seth, but he had to know that if he fired, he'd kill his own friend. Jay would have taken that shot back in the army, when he spent significant time on the firing range, but it would have been tough even then.

"Listen," Jay shouted, "everyone just put down the weapons! It's not too late!"

The kid at the window pivoted and pointed his weapon at Jay. "We told you to be quiet!"

"You could stop this rather than die! You're not really criminals, and you don't have a cause to die for. Is that how worthless you think your lives are?"

The kid at the window kept the gun trained on Jay. He'd never be able to hit Seth, but Jay he wouldn't be able to miss. "No cause? The Archangels thought they were so important. They treated us like dirt."

"And how many kids treated you like dirt?" Jay said. "A hundred? Are you going to kill a hundred kids? A thousand?"

"You're losers," Seth snarled. "And now you're losers with guns. I'll clean the streets before I let you kill anyone else."

Seth tightened his lock on Eric, whose nose streamed blood over Seth's forearm.

"Seth, stop, you're not helping!" Jay had no idea how to diffuse this. "They can turn it around—look at me!"

"Not them," Seth said. "They're street kids and criminals."

"So was I!" Jay cried out. "I was a gang member and a criminal!"

Seth said, "Not like them."

Jay's voice got frantic. "I did worse than they ever have! God can forgive anything!"

Seth tightened his grip on Eric and slipped his finger into the trigger. "There's no forgiveness for monsters like him."

Mike shouted, "That's not true! My dad was in a gang, and he went to Father Jay for confession! Father Jay forgave him!"

The kid at the window exclaimed, "That's it, everyone dies!" and squeezed the trigger.

The report rang off the cinderblock walls, and Jay flung himself over Esai. He could hear a kid screaming.

Seth. Seth, no, please...

Then loud police commands filled the room, voices ordering all guns down, and when Jay looked up, the kid from the window lay twitching on the classroom floor, his rifle flung aside. One of the entry team officer rushed toward him to remove the taser leads. The SWAT sharpshooter had tasered him from the doorway.

Seth still had the gunman in a headlock, but his gun was unfired. Seth released his hold on Eric, and a cop took the gun from his hand.

A SWAT officer pushed Jay aside and waved in one of the paramedics.

"This is Esai Marcovski. He needs emergency care," Jay said, but one of the tactical medical team members was already calling instructions into his radio.

It was so hard for Jay to get to his feet, but when he did, he found himself face to face with Kevin.

He couldn't move. Kevin wore headgear and body armor and had his gun in his hand. Clutching one of those stupid towelettes with blood all over his hands, Jay had never in his life felt more like a civilian.

Kevin said nothing, like a spring coiled tight enough to shoot all the way into space. Rage. Fear.

Then Seth ran to Jay. Ran and fell against him and sobbed into his shirt, and Jay turned to the kid and held him with someone else's blood covering them both.

Kevin reached into Jay's pocket and pulled out the radio, then snapped it off. Jay closed his eyes. Too much. There was too much to deal with right now.

The entry team evacuated the students while paramedics triaged the injured. Masa. Esai. The art teacher. And now the gunman from the window. A kid whose name Jay didn't even know, who lay on the floor while the police ordered him not to move.

Mike and Eric were cuffed for removal. The youngest, Tim, had met the cops in the stairwell and had surrendered rather than fire.

Kevin walked over to one of the SWAT members. He spoke into his radio, then approached Jay and Seth.

Jay said to Kevin, "Are you going to arrest Seth too?"

"We're bringing him to the station house." Kevin had his voice under control. It helped. Jay could listen to him taking charge and relax. "They'll ask him questions, but we have the audio proving he wasn't part of the attack." Kevin looked at the kid. "You should have stayed downstairs."

Kevin didn't snipe at Jay, *And you should have stayed downstairs too*. There was enough anger in his eyes to light a bonfire, so Jay spoke to Seth. "And you really shouldn't have taken Ben's gun. I wanted you to be safe."

Seth choked. "I couldn't just wait there. It was—"

Kevin said, "Your father a good man and a fine officer. You'll make one too, but seriously, you need to learn when to follow orders."

Kevin waved over one of the other officers and asked them to take Seth down to the captain. That done, Kevin looked right at him.

Jay said, "I'm sorry."

There should have been relief, but relief was a light year from here. So Jay just went over to the sink and washed his hands until the water ran pink, then clear, and then finally he left them in place with the stream rushing over them.

Esai, he prayed. *Seth. God, all these kids. Please.*

He turned, and Kevin was still waiting.

"You're an idiot," Kevin said.

Jay closed his eyes. "Thank you. You put up with a lot."

Finally Kevin hugged him. Then he said, "Go. You've got kids to take care of."

Authoritative and defeated at once. Jay nodded, and Kevin returned to the entry team commander.

Jay scanned the room. The kid from the window was being transferring him to a stretcher, his shirt torn where the taser barbs had penetrated. Although the medics had cut the leads, the barbs remained embedded in his skin. Kind of like sin. It went in easy but then took divine surgery to get it out again.

Leaning over him, Jay said, "You're in a lot of trouble, but hold still for a moment." He anointed the kid and murmured a blessing.

"Why'd you do that?" the boy whispered. "Am I going to die?"

"No," Jay squeezed his hand. "You're going to live."

Sixteen

Kevin hesitated on the rectory steps, but Holly walked right up and rang the bell. *Maybe this isn't a good idea,* he thought, but he didn't have one better.

Jay hadn't returned to the apartment after the incident. He'd hitched a ride over to the city hospital with one of the ambulances, and later on he'd texted Kevin to say he was needed at the rectory.

Needed, always needed somewhere else.

Holly, unwilling to just abandon their movie night, had opted instead to move it. So Kevin had gone home, packed Jay's bags, and here they were.

One of the upstairs boys yanked open the door as though it were a challenge, then recognized Holly. "Hey! Farrell! It's for you!"

Kevin followed her inside, carrying the duffle bag and that stack of research books and the thing Jay had called Mass-in-a-Box. Jay met them on the stairs, so he must have been up with the boys, and Holly rushed up to give him a hug. "Any news?"

"Esai's stable right now." From how tortured Jay looked, though, Kevin would have guessed otherwise. "I stayed until they kicked me out, but he's hanging in there. Social services is involved too, and they're having a field day with his relatives. The way the social worker was ranting, I may end up with custody or something."

Holly let go, saying, "You need a night off."

Jay shook his head. "The kids are really rattled. I don't want to leave them alone."

Holly said, "We're bringing movie night *to you*, silly. We've got five pizzas coming."

Kevin called up the steps, "I'll bring your stuff downstairs."

"Thank you." Jay looked pale. "Thank you, really."

Kevin put the bag on Jay's bed, but he left the books on his desk along with the Mass-in-a-Box. A bare bulb hung over a treadmill in an unfinished corner. And to the side was a litter box and a pair of bowls.

Back on the main floor, two of the house boys were hauling a television up the steps. Jay watched from the landing. "Holly brought all the Iron Man movies," he said.

"*My* Iron Man movies," Kevin said.

"You like Iron Man?" Jay looked surprised. "I'd have figured Captain America."

"I'm the Cap fan," Holly called from the kitchen. "Can this relationship be saved?"

When the boys got the TV upstairs, Kevin followed them to a bedroom where they'd crammed a bunch of mattresses, and the kids were calling their friends. Masa and Esai were conspicuously missing, but Seth was camped out in the corner.

Kevin said, "He isn't staying much longer, you know."

Jay looked up, startled. "Is he in trouble?"

Kevin shook his head. "We got his aunt and uncle on the phone today. They've lawyered up and are flying in tomorrow for an emergency hearing. I know the judge, and she's not going to take kindly to what the grandparents have done, assuming they even show."

Jay sighed. "That's a relief. He needs so much more than we can provide here."

"You gave him a family."

"We gave him a reason to reenact his parents' death and possibly die in the process." Jay withered under the weight of his own conscience. "Not quite the generosity I wanted to embody." He shook his head. "The phones have been insane today. Everything's off the hook right now, and we've all got our phones off, but there were even reporters showing up at the rectory before. I told everyone to donate something to their local homeless shelter, so maybe there will be some good."

He dropped to the mattress and settled against the wall. The doorbell rang, and boys flooded down the stairs to fetch the pizza. Holly followed with her wallet to pay for the things.

Kevin said, "So really, the only question I have after all this is, are you stupid?"

"I'm pretty sure I've cornered the market on that." Jay said, grinning as though at a private joke. "The bishop said, *Figure out your priorities,* and thanks to this, now I have."

The cat walked into the room and sat in a corner near the TV, presumably so no one would sit near it but everyone would be looking in its general direction.

Kevin said, "And after all your priestly discernment and near-death experiences, your decided your priority was keeping the cat?"

Jay laughed helplessly. "It's easier than not keeping the cat, trust me. The kids wanted to give it a name, and they kept arguing, so finally I just started reciting the saints of the Roman Canon." He smirked. "They wanted Damian because it reminded them of a demon in a movie, but I made them settle for Cosmos."

The cat gave a desultory lick of his black fur, and Kevin figured that was as close as they'd ever get to feline assent.

"I still don't know how I'm going to get everything done," Jay continued, "but after the sacraments—the kids are most important. Without them, there won't be any church."

Kevin said, "*These* kids are the future of the church?"

"Absolutely." Either Jay missed the sarcasm or else he didn't want to engage. "That's why I need to be at their sides, working with them, guiding them, living alongside them. And that means strengthening their families as well. That means being here to spot their pain before it consumes their souls."

Kevin leaned back against the wall. "That's seminary-talk."

"No, *this* is seminary-talk: God's taken care of everything else for me. He'd been telling me all along, and I was stubborn and never listened. You should be used to that," Jay said, giving Kevin the side-eye. "God found money for us when we needed it. He found people to take over all the little tasks. I can step back from the meetings and trust God will find more people to volunteer. This afternoon I recruited this one pain-in-the-behind legalistic parishioner and asked him to serve as volunteer trainer and coordinator. The guy's ecstatic." Jay chuckled ruefully. "Remember when I was talking to Holly about not being able to work your way into Heaven? Well, I can't work other people into Heaven either. My job is to hold open the door. But the one job I can't hand off to anyone else is to be me for the kids."

And so it came down to this, the moment of truth. Jay wasn't leaving. This was the new normal—Jay's new forever. Kevin reached into his pocket. "So you're going to be God's doorman?"

Jay smiled. "I like that. Yeah, I want to be God's doorman."

Kevin pulled out the thin metal circle. "Well, then you need this."

Jay's eyes lit up when Kevin handed over Mom's wedding ring. "You found it!" He laughed, but his hands were trembling enough that Kevin had to help him get the ring on his finger again. "I'd given up hope. I asked at the desk every day, but no one had seen it. You went back and looked again?"

Kevin didn't have to answer because a flood of boys trooped up the stairs. Among them was Masa, his arm swathed in bandages. "Yo, man! You were great in there! A total soldier!"

"Wow," Jay murmured, "just like I was trained or something."

"Hah! And, hey, look, it's my mom!" Masa laughed. "I told her about the movie, but she came for the pizza."

Jay slid closer to Kevin to make room. "Come on in and pull up a mattress." Mrs. Masa's Mom came in, looking pale but holding a loaded paper plate. One of the boys turned on the movie, and Holly brought in slices for Jay and Kevin.

Holly snuggled up next to Kevin. "You're so tense," she said. "Let Iron Man save the world tonight. You've had enough heroics for one day."

Kevin looked at Jay, focusing intently on a TV screen he couldn't see well and turning the wedding ring on his hand. He looked then at Seth, sprawled across the mattress on his last night in the house. "Maybe you're right," he said to Holly, squeezing her closer. "Maybe it's time for a different heroism."

THANK YOU!

Thank you so much for reading about Jay and Kevin!

I would really appreciate it if you could take the time to leave a review. Reviews help other readers decide whether to invest their energies in a story. They don't need to be five-paragraph book reports discussing the book's themes and symbolism. Just a couple of sentences and a star rating might help someone make up her mind. Think about what you would have liked to know prior to starting the book.

A number of people helped in the production of this book. I'd like to thank Sarah Begg, Laura Colon, and Susan Peek for giving feedback on the early versions, and also Margaret Keady Kalb for providing Cosmos his name (and the rationale thereof.) Thanks to Heather Turner of Versor Editing for her proofreading prowess, and thanks again to Charlotte Volnek for another incredible cover. I gasped when I saw what she'd come up with and how perfectly it encapsulated the story's emotions.

If you'd like to hear from me, I've got a mailing list at http://eepurl.com/bcnCNX. Or check out all my stories at http://janelebak.com/my-books/

If you liked Jay and Kevin's snarky banter, you might also like Lee and Bucky's. Laced with puns, riddled with quips, and set against the backdrop of New York City as the world's biggest playground, *Honest and for True* is just your everyday auto mechanic gal and the guardian angel only she can see.